MOOSE'S LAW

A Doug "Moose" McCrae Story

Jonathan Brown

MOOSE'S LAW
Copyright © 2019 by Jonathan Brown

All rights reserved. This book or any portion thereof may not be reproduced or used in any manner whatsoever without the express written permission of the author except for the use of brief quotations in a book review.

Edited by Elaine Ash

Cover by Karen Phillips/PhillipsCovers.com

ISBN: 978-0-9885442-4-6

DEDICATION

For my parents, "Mommabell" n "Daddy-o!"
We did it!

Other books by Jonathan Brown:

The Big Crescendo…A Lou Crasher Mystery
(release date 2019)

Don't Shoot The Drummer…A Lou Crasher Mystery
(release date 2020)

*A Boxing Trainer's Journey…
A Novel Based on the Life of Angelo Dundee*

Kanu…A Boy's Journey
(audio children's book ages 5-9: contact through website)

Moose Hunt
(working title, coming soon)

Contact:
jonathanbrownwriter.com
jonathanbbooks@Instagram.com
jonathanbrownwriter@Facebook.com

*There is no greater agony
than bearing an untold story inside you.*

Maya Angelou

MOOSE'S LAW

A Doug "Moose" McCrae Story

Jonathan Brown

Saturday three a.m. I lock up the nightclub and head down the alley to my truck. At work I break up fights, check ID cards, clear aisles for servers and troubleshoot for my inept boss. I'm an over-aged bouncer. I should have left the job years ago, yet I stay.

By three-twenty I'm home. Leftover spaghetti with a beer chaser is my ritual. I look forward to this point all week long.

I hit the rack by four with high hopes of sleeping late. Thirty minutes deep, a woman's shriek jolts me up. She practically sounds in the room with me. I hop out of bed and flip the shades. The vision chills me out.

A woman; young, fit, is fighting for her life against four large pit bulls. My Glock 17 is on the bedside table. I check it on the run. Diving out the front door, I start to sprint.

"HEY!" Shouting does nothing to distract the dogs.

I can't get a shot—too risky. She's being mauled and putting up a hell of a fight. I get up close and put the muzzle to the head of an albino-colored dog with a few scattered black spots. Decide against pulling the trigger. The bullet could roll around in that skull and come out who knows where. Or it might pass right through the ear and into this poor woman. Plan B: I pull the dog by a hind leg, lift it up and fire two quick shots. The dog doesn't let up. He wriggles and begins violently torquing his head back and forth in a death shake, the way they do when they kill creatures large and small. Repositioning my barrel, I aim for something vital and fire. *Thwump.* The staccato boom from the gun is muffled due to the beast's thick body cavity, making it sound like a cannon fired from a distant shore. The violent torquing stops. I pull the body off her ankle and toss the carcass away.

One down, three to go.

A tan-colored animal has a nasty hold of the woman's other leg. She's giving everything she has—doesn't know the meaning of the word 'quit.' A battle-scarred second dog has a grip on her shoulder near the bicep. I'm glad it's not near the throat, but he might get the idea soon.

The last animal has the full albino gene. He's got a grip on her hip. The shoulder dog lets go and eyes her neck. I shove the gun in her hand.

"Shoot that one," I shout, pointing to the albino. I leap at the dog going for the throat kill.

I grab the thick neck with both hands and drag him away. Then I lift him high and slam him down hard on the pavement. The beast gives out a sharp cough, but is far from done. It rushes me. I hear my gun go off —two quick pops. Out of my peripheral, the smallest dog goes limp.

Two down, two to go.

My opponent leaps at me. With a meaty hand I bat it to the ground. I used to slam offensive linemen upside their helmets in my football days the same way. Two hundred and eighty pounds back then, I run at about two-fifty-five now, but can still lay the smack down. I'm downright surgical with the open palm. It's a good technique at work. Saves breaking fingers and knuckles.

The dog attempts to gather itself. I get down and wrap my pythons around his neck from behind, constricting like a boa. This time, when I bring him down, I come with him so that he hits the pavement at a grotesque angle. SNAP! His spine gives out. Two vertebrae poke through his fur into my gut.

My gun goes off three more times. The tan animal goes possum, but still the girl shrieks all kinds of hell. She's propped on her elbows shaking slightly—shock. The dead dog's mouth is still around her shinbone. I move quickly, fearing the animal's jaw may lock up from muscle spasm. I work, prying the big-headed dog's mouth off. We get lucky, no spasm. The grip is easy to remove.

Her ankle leaks like a sieve. A chunk of flesh is flipped off the side of her calf. I figure a dog ripped her, but looking closer, it looks like a bullet sheared the flesh. She's either shot herself, or the bullet ricocheted off the dog's thick skull. I rip off my t-shirt and tie the calf off, ebbing the flow for the time being. She grimaces but takes it.

Neighbors start coming out of their houses. They watched our bloodbath and now feel the coast is clear. Sirens inbound meet my ears.

"What's yo' name, baby?"

"Al… Alexandra."

"Alexandra, ya gonna be okay. Help is on the way."

"It's César… he…"

"Where is César? César who?"

"Van Nuys…" Her lids come down and then open.

"Here, lean yo' head back. I apologize, ya gonna to have to lay back on my bare leg. I sleep in boxers."

She doesn't protest.

Her eyes open and close again, only more slowly this time. I'm probably a massive black blurry vision with a deep voice to her.

"What are you sayin'? Say it again, Alexandra."

The sirens get louder. The first response vehicle comes in; a paramedic bus. They get out and hustle over—one white female, one white male, both just south of twenty-five years old.

The woman comes straight for us and joins me on the pavement. The young male freezes and stares at the scene. I'm not sure what the big deal is until I look at it from his perspective: Four dead muscled pit bulls, a large black man in boxers—and a slender Latina bleeding out.

I run the injuries down for them before handing Alexandra over. Then I cruise dog to dog noticing several scars, old lacerations and puncture wounds. Either these dogs were abused, or used in the underground fight world. I find what I'm looking for on the fourth animal, a dog tag. I rip it off just as two black and whites barrel onto the scene.

"Officers," my voice booms. "I gotta Glock 17 and a permit up in my home." I point, remaining on my knees. "My gun was used defending this woman who was attacked by these dogs."

I keep the boom in my voice. I want as many witnesses as possible on the pavement to hear my words. A black man of my dimensions with a gat can be recipe for nervous rollers.

"I'm putting the piece, sorry, the gun... down."

Of one accord, the cops, their guns, and onlookers with phones all aim at yours truly in the same moment.

"Don't move!"

"Wouldn't dream of it."

A young black kid laughs from behind his smart phone.

A black woman in her early sixties calls, "I'm filming your every move, officers, so y'all better be careful, now."

"Thanks, Greta," I bellow.

"You're welcome, Moose."

The kid laughs again. An Asian cop gently kicks my gun back and behind her. I get pushed flat for a pat-down. I'm clean and co-operate, so after that, guns are holstered and I'm allowed to get to my feet. They don't return my gat right away. After being escorted to my crib and satisfying them my permit is legit, I'm given my gun and a visit to the paramedic vehicle. No bites are visible but I opt to take the tetanus shot. The paramedic hastily hands me a piece of gauze and instructs me to hold it over the pinhole where a trickle of blood escapes. They're anxious to hustle Alexandra off to the hospital, which is good—she needs them more than I do.

Before I can head back inside the house, a stocky Latino cop approaches.

"Doug 'Moose' McCrae?"

"We know each other, officer?"

"I was a big fan. What happened, Moose? I was looking forward to watching you on any given Sunday in the NFL."

"What can I say? Huge on potential, light on talent."

"Modest."

"Modest Moose, that's me." I was a defensive tackle in my college days. I stepped up and made big plays when we needed them. But consistency? Well, not so much. For reasons unbeknownst to me I developed a following.

He extends a hand. I wipe my hand on my boxers before we shake. "Nice work with the girl. She could have died." The ambulance pulls out at a good clip.

Inside the house, I still have the dog tag in my paw. I put it on my kitchen table and go to shower the blood and everything else off before a few hours of shut-eye.

I check myself in the bathroom mirror. Scratches, bruises, and my shoulder which has never healed right from the gridiron days, nags a bit more than usual. Overall, this is nothing compared to the feeling on a Sunday after a football game when I was younger. Although, at thirty-five, I know the current soreness will get to me as days pass. Under the massaging hot water, I think about the tag and how I should have turned it over to the cops—let them do what they're paid to. But I'm running point on this one. I do that sometimes.

❖ ❖ ❖

I sleep longer than planned but there's still time for coffee and a quick power shake. My trusty Ford F250 King Ranch gets me to Silverlake Medical without any problem.

"Alexandra, you don't look so bad," I lie. "How're ya feeling?"

Alexandra struggles to prop herself up against hospital-issue pillows. She winces but manages a faint smile. "It's you. I didn't think I'd see you again."

Her right arm is bandaged from wrist to elbow. Splotches of red show through the gauze in three places. Her other arm is in a sling. Her eyes have a strong light to them—the fire of a fighter. They're a lighter shade of brown than I remember and much softer—including the one with the solid-red subconjunctival hemorrhage, the medical term for broken blood vessel. I received more than a few of them during football. Dirty players live by the eye poke. Her right leg is thickly wrapped and slightly elevated.

"I don't know how to thank you."

"Ya just did. Name's Doug but e'body calls me Moose."

She smiles, "Well, thank you so much, Moose." She extends a bandaged hand. I shake as gently as I can manage with my big mitt.

"Don't know if you remember, but you mentioned the name 'César.'"

Her faint smile disappears.

"I like gettin' straight to the point," I say, holding up a 'relax' hand. "So, tell me, where I can find César? I want to have a chat with him."

With a look of concern, she pushes herself back into the pillows and sits up taller. No doubt she's nervous about a big-ass brother sitting at the end of her bed, forcing his way into her life.

"Why do you want to talk to César?"

"Because I'm chatty like that."

Her raven-colored hair drapes over her toned shoulders. Either she or a nurse has brushed it out, or maybe she just woke up like that. Long thick natural lashes go with her light browns. She's beautiful, verging on stunning... and that's in her current ass-kicked state.

I do my best not to imagine her all cleaned up. Need to stay focused.

"Why are you helping me? Honestly."

"It ain't about money or sex or anything like that, trust me. But any dude who'd set four killer pits on a woman—" I stop myself as I notice her wide-eyed look staring at my big mitt now balled into a fist. "The dude deserves a chat, Alexandra."

"Because you're chatty," she says, forcing a smile.

I nod. "You live in Silverlake?"

"Yes."

"And ya mentioned Van Nuys—he live there?"

"Yes."

"That means he transported the animals all that way… for you."

She shrugs her shoulders.

"This dude drove four deadly pits fifteen miles in the middle o' the night to attack you and wake the sleeping Moose. Hmm."

"I'm sorry we woke you," she says with a smile, but it's forced. Her attempt at being upbeat fails to hide her fear.

A slender black nurse with a sunshiny smile comes by and says Alexandra will be released in a day or so. The doctor needs to be satisfied she's okay.

◆ ◆ ◆

The dog's name is Chico, or should I say *was* Chico, and at one time he lived in Canoga Park. I lock the address into Google maps and roll out in my King Ranch. There's parking directly in front of the house. No need for subtlety. If this is César's home we get it on from the moment the door opens. I vault the front steps and rap three times on the security door. I have to do it loud since I'm competing with a Spanish telenovela coming from a TV inside the home. A savory aroma seeps from within. Makes my stomach rumble.

"Si?" It's an elderly Latina voice.

"Good morning, ah, *buenos dias*."

"Yes, can I help you?"

"Can you see this through the security screen?" I ask, holding up the dog tag.

"*Dios mio*," she says, unlocking the door and gently taking the tag from me. Her wrinkled face creases further as tears come to her eyes. "Chico."

"Chico was your dog?"

"*Si*, he go missing one year plus one half ago. Have you found him? Is he okay?"

"I'm sorry, ma'am, he's not okay. He was killed attacking a woman on the street."

With eyes full of water, she looks up at me.

"Attack? A wo—woman? *Es verdad?*"

"I bet Chico was a good dog. All dogs start that way," I say. "But somebody got hold of him and turned him... mean. Not his fault."

She nods slowly with unfocused eyes.

I realize this is a lot for this woman. I need to check myself, ease off the gas.

"Tell me about Chico, what was he like?"

"He was so loving and playful, never rough. He was *muy amable.*"

"Gentle."

"Si."

"What color was he?"

"Oh, he was a beautiful golden brown. *Mi pobre Chico*," she says, wiping a tear away from her eye. She'd just referred to the dog Alexandra was forced to shoot... with my gun. I give her a moment to visit the memory stirring in her unfocused eyes.

She clutches her throat as if a pearl necklace were around her neck.

"Does the name César mean anything to you?"

"No," she says, crossing her body. "Did he take my Chico?"

"Looks that way. And I believe he uses dogs in fighting pits." I pause. "Among other things."

"I believe you Mister—?"

"McCrae, but people call me Moose. And yo' name is?"

"Graciella. Gracias, *Señor* Moose, wait, *un momento*." She hurries back into her apartment and comes out with a napkin, holding two tamales. "Here, for you."

My stomach rumbles again. A man my size ain't much for turning down good food.

"*Para ti. Tu es grande*. Big man."

I gently take the napkin as if handling a baby bird.

"This smells incredible. Thank you. *Gracias*."

I take a large bite and feel savory juice dripping down my chin. She snickers politely and hands me more napkins to go. By the time I reach my truck both tamales are history. I make a mental note to put in extra time on the heavy bag next workout. Also, this César dude ain't just a scumbag dog fighter, he's a thief, turning other people's pets lethal instead of breeding his own. What the hell is Alexandra doing mixing with a guy like that?

❖ ❖ ❖

Back home, I put a pot of coffee on and pull up the YouTube icon on my tablet. A Scottish fiddler in full regalia from beret to kilt-and-spoor fills the screen. Gavin Macdonald is a Scottish Fiddler and my go-to guy. His instructional videos are the best. I open my beat-up hutch, reach behind the instructional violin books and pull the case out. I used to leave the fiddle on the stand so I could admire it during the day. But in this 'hood the fiddle would be the first thing gone in a break-in, even though she was purchased for cheap at a Hollywood pawnshop.

I pop the nylon-covered plywood case and sniff the ancient aroma from the black velvet insides. The case has two bow compartments, but I have only one bow, which is slightly shorter than standard. I tell myself this will aid my speed. I pick her up and set the fingers of my left hand in place. Normally, I'd warm up with the scales but this morning's events have put me behind schedule. There's nothing like time with a fiddle to let the subconscious go to work on sortin' through a mess.

I turn up the sound and sink into the first verse at a very slow tempo. My fingering is wrong. The sound of two cats fighting at night fills the room. *Screeeeeee. Scrawwww.* I hit pause after three measures, feeling like I should apologize to the fiddle. I shake out my hands and stretch my wrists. Clearly, I need to warm up with scales—the price o' doin' good music—no shortcuts.

The coffee finishes perking. I pour a half cup, black, and take a hit. Back at the tablet I replay Gavin and go at the song again. I first heard *Going Home* at my Scottish grandmother's funeral. The tune was played on a fiddle by one of the most beautiful auburn-haired women I'd ever laid eyes on. Her version of the song nearly stopped my heart. The day after grandma went into the ground, I bought the old fiddle. I also inherited her house, this little bungalow.

I go through the first half of the song for another twenty minutes, then call it. The last half of the song is a mess but I'll get there.

❖ ❖ ❖

As I'm about to head out the door to work there's a knock at my door. I open it and see the stocky Latino cop and somewhat fan of my football career from the dog attack.

"Officer."

"Moose, ya got a quick minute?"

"Sure, come on in. A minute I can spare."

Ortiz is a uniform cop, which means he isn't a detective. Maybe he's just thorough—trying to move his career forward. I respect that.

He comes in and takes in as much of my apartment as he can before getting to the point. I don't offer him coffee, water or even a chair—I have to get to work.

"I'll get right to it," he says. "I wonder if there's anything else you can tell me about the attack."

"Like what?" I wonder if he knows about the tag. If he knows, he's going to have to ask me. I'm playin' that one close until then.

"Was there anything else you remember or saw?" Ortiz pauses. "Or did?"

He either knows something or is purely suspicious of me. I have to give him something but I'll take the long way around.

"You wondering if I knew the woman on the pavement? The answer is no. This was just a random attack outside my door."

He pulls out a notepad and jots down a few lines.

"There was one thing."

He looks up from his pad, "Oh?"

"These dogs were abused or more 'n likely used for fighting. They looked like a sushi chef had sliced 'em up."

"You're right on the fighting part. The ears and tails were chopped. Not by a vet either."

"The significance?"

"Animals read cues off each other: wagging tail—happy, ears perked—nonthreatening. Like the way we read facial expressions."

"Dog owners seek every advantage then, huh?"

He nods.

"That adds."

He moves his attention back to the notepad but stops himself.

"Did you hear or see any vehicles moving in the area at the time of the attack?"

I give myself a moment. The memory is vague on it.

"Reason I ask is a neighbor down the block saw a truck tearing down the street with speed. Time line coincides."

"It'd make sense. Them dogs were brought in 'cause these animals weren't from this 'hood. Any neighbor'll tell you that."

He holds my look the way cops do when reading someone, then goes back to the notepad.

"Witness said the truck was dark-colored, large, with big tires and raised up. She couldn't place the make and didn't get a plate." He flips the pad closed.

"Sorry officer, it all went down so fast."

Ortiz runs a hand through his hair and sighs. He's fatigued, but that's the job. He appears to search his mind for more questions. So, I jump in.

"What'll ya do with the dog cadavers?"

"Animal control will destroy them. That's what usually happens."

He seems like he's going to say more but holds up, so I push.

"Usually? Something different this time around?"

"The dogs are going to be autopsied. Sergeant wants to know if there are any clues on the animals—DNA, whatever, that will lead us to the owner. Besides, the vet's going to be in there anyway, pulling the slugs from your gun so… why not see what else may be in there?"

"Makes sense. Any chance you could hip me to what they find?"

His face says I pushed too far.

"Why would you want to know, Moose? Are you—"

It was time to remind him he was once a fan of mine. "When I played football it was all 'bout the team. Any fool that focused on his own stats wudn't worth shit. It was 'bout the guys in the locker-room, the guys on the field. That night outside my crib, me and that woman…we became a team. She fired my gun. We killed animals intent on killin' us. We won," I suck down some air. "And they lost. My curiosity is all about that woman 'cause for a moment in time she was my teammate. It's just the way us players are wired."

He keeps hard eyes on me. Never went to the notepad once during my ramble. Finally, he folds up the pad and tucks it away. He heads for the door. I open it.

"I may be in touch, no promises."

I watch him walk down my steps, climb in his cruiser and pull away from the curb. I toss my jacket on, kill the lights and lock up. I get ten feet from my truck when a thought hits me like an eighteen-wheeler. Greta, my neighbor, was snapping pictures of everything when the cops showed. But I know Greta, and I'd bet my fiddle she'd been taping from the first howl out of poor Alexandra. Greta's *that* neighbor.

I walk three houses over, climb her dilapidated steps and knock on the door. She answers in a long cream housecoat, slippers to match and her hair up in a scarf. She may be working on a dye job. My nostrils flare out as a succulent cooking smell wafts out the open door.

Her eyes smile first before her mouth follows suit. "Greta's world famous spareribs. You in, Moose?"

"Dang, that smells good, but I can't. I'm late for work. I got one question for you, though."

"Well, you'll ask it in here. I don't talk in doorways."

I step in and take a full inhale of the ribs. I'm in trouble. Greta closes the door behind us. I hear three locks bolt home. She walks past, slipping her phone into my hand and continues to the kitchen. I follow.

"The code is 1234. Hit the camera icon, you'll see what you came for."

I sit at her kitchen table and follow instructions. Greta knows a lot more than people give her credit for, she's always one step ahead. She plops a plate of ribs down in front of me. I lose focus on the phone and reach for the ribs. Greta slaps my hand.

"Work first. I know you're running this dog business down, Moose, now stay the course for godsakes. We need to police ourselves."

"Yes ma'am," I say, and look at her photos.

"If you don't find whoever sicced those dogs on that woman, this joint will have a reputation for being soft. You need to see this through, Moose."

"That's the plan, Greta."

As I suspected, Greta's photos began from her curtained window, into her yard and out into the street. I search for the truck the cop told me about and find it on the eighth picture. After things got serious, she switched to video. Seeing the replay tells me one thing: Alexandra and I were very lucky to come out on top.

"There you are."

"What?" she asks. I hand her the phone.

"The truck in the background. The one moving away."

"I didn't like that, someone rolling away from a scene like that," she says.

"Did you show this to the cops or tell them about the truck?"

She puts her eyes on me—the outside of her gray irises show early signs of cataracts. "We need to police ourselves," she says sternly. *"Now* you can eat your ribs."

"Got to take 'em to go," I say, rising. She grabs me a stack of napkins.

At the door, "Greta I gotta share this with the cop that just braced me."

"The hell you will." She scowls at me.

"Look, he's on our side. Judgin' character is my thing, Greta, trust me. 'Sides, if I don't give him something, I can't be the police you want round here. He'll shut me down real quick. Send me those pics, Greta, please."

By the end of my block I'm done with the ribs and forced to use every napkin in the stack.

❖ ❖ ❖

I take the back alley to the club. Rap three times hard on the double steel doors, slide my hands into my coat pockets and wait. My phone vibrates. Greta's sent the photos.

Half a minute passes before I hear the bolt-lock mechanism. The door swings out and Curly, the Mohawk-sporting bar manager, pokes his head out.

"S'up Moose?"

I step past Curly. The door locks automatically behind us.

"Ready to rock?" I ask, moving to the bar. He gives me a thumbs-up.

I grab a tub of lemons and limes out of the fridge and bring them to the counter. Then I grab a cutting board and my favorite paring knife and set to work. This is bartender work, but I always do it. I find it relaxing for some reason. Only this time, I'm not relaxed. My thoughts continue to drift to Alexandra. I wonder how the sadistic bastard did it. Did he kick her out of the truck and give her, what, a ten-second head start? Did he laugh to himself as the first animal dragged her to the pavement? And what does he do when the big brother leaps into the fight? He flees... like a coward.

❖ ❖ ❖

The doors open at eight and the place is jammed an hour later. As head bouncer, I roam the place by making stops by the front door, bar, and occasionally at the boss's office—he likes updates even though he watches everything with the eye-in-the-sky security camera system. The night is no different from usual.

Brittney approaches with a no-nonsense look on her face. Flawless mocha skin. Hair in a ponytail to one side. Pencil skirt with black tights and a thick stitch down the back, accentuating shapely legs. She puts her tray down on the ledge beside me.

"I got a creepy fucker asking questions about you, Moose."

"Oh?"

"He just asked if you're head of security. I don't like his look or his vibe. This is his beer, ya got a minute to come check him out?"

I start to follow her through the crowd. Dave, another bouncer, interrupts our trek.

"Moose, we got a purse snatcher. Ran into the ladies."

"Specifically, the ladies?"

He nods. Three weeks ago contractors added a third bathroom—three separate doors. Doors one and two have the classic stick figures for man or woman. Door number three is marked "All Gender" and has a stick figure half-man, half-woman. That's why I had to ask "specifically."

"Brit, I gotta handle this. Get a pic if you can. Run the voice-record on your phone and get the conversation. Get him talking. Answer whatever he asks 'bout me. Just make sure ya bullshit him."

"Done and done, hon,'" she says, turning on her heel.

I turn back to Dave. "He still have the purse?"

"As far as we know. Guys up front say he might be packing. Something small like a twenty-five or something. He fast tho'. Usain Bolt fast."

"And they let him in carrying heat?" I say it not expecting an answer. "Let's go."

❖ ❖ ❖

I tell the bouncers, Dave and Ronnie, to wait outside the door and grab him if he slips by. I open the door and peek my head in the ladies' room. A woman on stilettos hurries quickly toward me. I open the door wider and guide her out.

"Any other women inside?"

"No, and the prick is in the last stall."

"Thanks," I say, and hand her over to Dave.

Stepping inside, I enter the closest stall then call out, "Hey bud, I understand you got somethin' don't belong to you."

"This is the ladies room get the fuck out of here," a voice responds.

"We'll go together, how's that?"

"Fuck you!"

"Come on, bud, gimme a break," I call. "Drop the purse and walk away clean. My boss is up my ass on this one."

"Good," he says and fires two quick shots. That means he has four more shots unless he has some sort of modified magazine. I doubt it. I put my right hand on top of the stall door, and my left on the side, and rip the door off the hinges.

"What the hell is that?" the voice calls. I can tell he's come out of the stall to take a look.

I leap out, holding the door in front of my body and charge. TING! TING! TING! The door dimples with a bullet at my chest height. I get three more steps when two dimples come near my shoulder. His final shot goes high into the ceiling above me, then I hear the click-click of the empty gun. He screams as the door hits and pancakes him against the back wall with the full-length mirror. I drop the door. He's slumped on the floor out cold. The mirror is cracked at his head height.

I pick up the twenty-five with a paper towel and put it in my pocket. The purse lays on the floor with articles strewn around the toilet. I gather the belongings and put them back in the purse, then check the ID. It's a California driver's license. The name is Sandra Lange, blonde, lives in Sherman Oaks and, judging by the date, she shouldn't be allowed in our club for another six months. I'll have to smack the guys up front for that.

Dave and Ronnie come in and stand beside me, looking the purse snatcher over.

"Mission accomplished, I see," Dave says.

"I'm like a Vegas casino. I always win." The gun goes from my pocket into Dave's hand. "Take this asshole to the office, sit on him and call the cops. I'm gonna find the girl."

Before they move, though, I motion them to wait. "Hang on." Reaching into the kid's pocket, I pull out some cash. Then I go into his wallet. There's cash there as well. All in, it totals seventy-five dollars.

"I wouldn't think that's your style," Dave says, concerned.

"It ain't. I'm gonna ask Sandra-the-snatchee how much she had in her purse. This guy had already cleaned it when I got here. Whatever her number is, I'll give her the money."

I'm nearly at the door when Ronnie asks, "What if the number is over seventy-five, like she bullshits you?"

"Then she gets nothing because she's underage. It's a little something called Moose's Law."

Sandra's standing with two young women about her age, doing their best to console her. She lights up when she sees the purse in my hand. I hold it out and she snatches it like a toddler would a favorite toy.

"Oh my god, thank you, thank you so much," she says, standing on her toes to give me a hug. She goes through and checks her belongings.

"Ah, where's my money? I had like forty-five bucks in here. And it wasn't even my money to—"

She lets out a sigh of relief as I peel off bills totaling forty-five dollars.

"Oh my god, you are so awesome. Can I, like, buy you a drink or something?" Her eyes are big, hazel and dime-shaped. Her friends smile at me as well.

"Sure, but you'll have to do it in about six months when you're twenty-one," I say, killing the vibe.

"I am twenty—"

"That's right, you're twenty. Come back on your birthday, ask for Moose, that's me. I'll waive the cover charge—might even buy you a shot."

"Oh, come on, can't we stay for, like, one drink?"

"Are you two ladies twenty-one? You can stay if you are."

The sideways glances and blushes tell me I don't have to check the other IDs. I escort them to the rear door.

"You ladies have a wonderful night."

"Not cool dude," one of them says to me. Sandra turns back and mouths the words 'thank you' to me and adds a wink with it.

When I turn from the back door, Brittney is waiting for me with a hand on her hip. She's not pleased.

"Is the guy still here?"

"No."

"Okay, whatta you got?" I ask.

"A photo worth shit, but the dialogue's good."

She holds out the phone, then pulls it back. "What's going on, Moose?"

"Let me check out what ya got, then I'll tell you everything."

She slowly hands me the phone. "Tell Dave I'm taking five."

"I want to hear it all, Moose."

I nod, then head to the cooler behind the bar and close the door. I know Brittney's code. I punch it, sit back and listen.

"Hi, nice night," the man says.

I hear sounds of the drink placed on the table.

"That'll be nine dollars." Pause. "Say, why were you asking about Eddie, my head bouncer?"

Brittney used the name Eddie instead of my name—nice.

"I dunno, I'm just saying he's a big guy. All your bouncers are."

"It's a big club, size matters. Will there be anything else?"

I can hear Brittney's annoyance. She manages to keep it cool, though.

"I'm just saying you've got some beefy dudes here, especially that big black Eddie guy roaming the floor. What's he like, six-four? Dang. He's like a big black shark swimmin' in a sea of losers out there."

I fully get Brittney's radar going off on this guy. My jaw clenches. The cooler door opens and Brittney comes in.

"Hey."

"Hey."

"You hear it all yet?" she asks.

"Almost. Can you describe this guy?"

"Gladly. Acne, lots on his cheeks, a thin mustache above his top lip, and the yellow-toothed grin of an asshole. The eyes were sharp blue. On most men that would be hot, but it doesn't work for him. Looks like he was spawned by a demon. The eyes were color contacts by the way. Creeped me out."

"I appreciate your attention to detail. Nationality?"

"Latino. I wanted to take my Ruger and shoot him in his canines, just for grinning the way he was."

Brittney takes a deep sip of her iced coffee. "Oh, and then he was sitting with his legs open the way guys do, but when I came back with the drink he spreads his legs wider, knowing I saw that shit. I'd like to shoot him square in the balls."

"Let me finish your tape." I hit the play button.

Brittney's voice comes on. "Do you want to meet him? Eddie I mean?"

"That'll happen, sweetheart, don't you worry. Say, does Eddie like cats? He doesn't seem like a dog lover to me."

"Sure cats, cars and karaoke that's our Eddie. Let me go get him. You'll love him."

"No!"

"He stands up and tosses ten bucks on the table, then knocks the Rolling Rock over," Brittney says.

"For the cleaning, he says. "Tell Eddie I'll see him around."

I hand the phone back to Brittney.

"Like I said, I couldn't get a good shot of him but I got the receipt of his credit card. She hands it over.-

❖ ❖ ❖

Back in the club, the song *Candy Shop* by 50 Cent booms through the giant EV speakers. We play a mix of light rap with radio-friendly lyrics and rock 'n roll. The dark mahogany bar top is loaded with cocktails, beers and elbows. Twenty-somethings attempting to hail the bartenders look like stockbrokers on the New York stock exchange floor. Instead of walking past the high-top tables that butt up against the DJ booth, I decide to cut through the dance floor toward the area where my admirer sat, see if he left any clues.

I descend the three steps to the dance floor. I can't remember how many times I've asked the boss to level the floor, which is a liability hazard for drunk dancers, and a nightmare for my security staff when it comes to removing an undesirable. I wade into the pool of dancers and carve a path. Halfway through the throng, my sixth sense goes haywire. Long ago I termed it bouncer's intuition.

Someone with bad intentions is close by and gunning for me. My head moves on a swivel like it did in my gridiron days. The music, which is back to rock 'n roll, thumps hard. I block it out. Bodies gyrate all around me. Do I keep moving or make a stand? A stand against who, though? I can't find the threat but I know it's near. I begin a quarter turn to my left and that's when I see it. Bottle, hand, tattoo on wrist, target—my face. I get a hand up just shy of too late.

Glass breaks over my hand and the back of my head. The couple closest to me notices and backs up. I turn and face the man Brittney has just described, right down to the yellow-toothed grin. Her description of him is better than ninety percent accurate. I give my head a shake. If he's worried the bottle had little effect, he doesn't show it. From somewhere on his person, he hauls out a double-bladed folding knife made by the TAK Company. I recognize the brand, having confiscated them off patrons in the past. The weapon is used more for slicing and slashing than stabbing—incredibly sharp. Just one nick to the right spot and this big brother will be bleeding out on the dance floor.

Customers catch on and move away. César comes in fast. He must know I have a cavalry not far off. Problem is, César is excellent with the blade. I can barely track it, but what I can track are his arm and shoulder movement and footwork. I consider taking off my blazer and wrapping it around my arm but I'd never have enough time, he's way too fast. He lunges forward and drops low for a thigh slice and nearly gets it done. I pull back just when he comes up with a backhanded swing for my face. I yank my head back and feel the back of my skull connect with a patron behind me. A girl screams as the patron hits the floor. I don't chance a glance. César's right-handed. Rather than move to his left like a boxer, I move side to side, constantly switching up my leading foot.

Where the hell is the cavalry?

César darts in high. I block the swing with the outside of my bicep and receive a slice on his retreat. Dave bursts through the onlookers. César sees this and quickly grabs the nearest kid, a one-hundred-and-twenty-pound nerd type, and takes him hostage.

"You don't want to do that, César," I shout over the music.

"Stay back," he yells, dragging the terrified kid toward the back exit. I look over his shoulder and see that Rolf, who is supposed to be stationed at the back door, is AWOL.

Dammit!

If César makes it to that door he'll be in the wind.

"Let him go, César. I wanna talk."

His grin tells me he doesn't buy it, which means he's smarter than he looks. All I want is to wrap my meats around his neck and squeeze until the color contacts pop out of his head. He makes it to the back door. The hostage is crying. I tell him it's going to be okay. With a heavy boot heel, César back-kicks the door open and briefly checks the alley.

"See ya 'round, *puto*," he spits, and gives the kid a four-inch slice to his cheek before kicking him in the back toward me. I catch the kid just as Dave appears. I hand the kid sideways to him.

"Take care of this, I'm going." I haul ass out the door.

Dave shouts after me, "We're not insured out there, Moose!"

"Don't care," I shout back, making a hard right down the alley. César has fifteen yards on me. I've dragged down dozens of quarterbacks in far better shape than César in my day. I can't go far, but the short explosive burst is my thing. He sneaks a look over his shoulder. His eyes reveal he regrets it because I gain on him. He accelerates. Forty yards on, we close on the end of the alley. He pulls ahead because he's running for his life and I'm just running to beat a man to illness.

At the mouth of the alley he takes a sharp left. I get there a few beats after him but he's gone, way up the street. My thirty-five-year-old tree-trunk thighs full of lactic acid call it a day. I have more stamina in me but I'm not about to get any faster. Panting, I bend and rest my hands on my knees. As I see him crest the hill and drop off, I feel a nagging at my right arm. I check and see he's not only ruined my jacket I'm leaking blood through the tear.

You're a dead man, César.

❖ ❖ ❖

Rolf is at the back door, where he should have been, when I get back. I give him a piece of my mind, then put my shoulder to his chest as I squeeze past. To my back he tells me two uniforms are in the office with the boss. I move to the cooler, grab two bar rags, and make a tourniquet. Pull my blazer back on.

The cops do their best to hide their boredom. I do my best to speak clearly and quickly, and wrap it up. My boss, Jason Grimes, is excited. I'm sure he'll tell his buddies tonight was non-stop action. I'm done in fifteen minutes. Cops take the shaken kid and blow. Grimes wants me to stick around. I take off my blazer and show him my wound.

"Done for the night, Grimes."

He protests to my back as I exit.

My phone buzzes as I ease the truck into a spot three doors down from my place. I don't recognize the number but pick up.

"Moose, you haven't been straight with me."

It's Officer Ortiz. I power down the truck and take the call there.

"What do you mean?"

"We got a call from your club."

"Yeah, purse snatcher," I say.

"I'm talking about a knife fight followed by foot pursuit in the streets by a large black guy fitting your description."

News travels fast. Customers with cell phones. My guys never would have let on I left the club.

"You're talkin' 'bout a typical weekend, man."

"Only young thrill-seeking bouncers go off-property. A veteran like you would stay home." He pauses. "Unless he was working something."

It wasn't an all-out accusation, there was some bait on the end of his fishhook. I decide to keep my lip buttoned.

"Gimme, Moose," he continues. "The knife wielder, he's connected to the dogs isn't he?"

"Look officer, I've been straight with you every step—"

"Cut the bullshit. I may be a fan but that doesn't mean I won't slap an obstruction charge on you. This is police business."

Clearly, the cop is invested and isn't going anywhere soon. If my grandma were here she'd say, "Moose, you best go along to get along. He's the Man. You're not."

"Okay, straight up, I've got something for you."

"I'm listening." Some of the anger leaves Ortiz's voice.

"I've got video. One of my neighbors hipped me to it."

"Still got my card?"

"Yeah."

"Email it over."

"Will do," I say, hoping to wrap this up.

"What will I be looking at?"

"Background. Truck you asked about. I'll bet my tiny-assed paycheck it's the dog owner's ride. He brought those animals to my block and gave the kill order." My jaw clenches as I say it.

Ortiz is quiet a moment. I imagine he's short-handing notes into his black pad.

Finally, "Is there a reason you didn't mention this when I stood in your goddamn living room?"

"Didn't have it then."

"Why didn't your neighbor share the video with us? We only canvassed the whole damn block."

"Trust. She's a civilian in the hood and you're cops. Do the math."

"I'm so tired of this damn rhetoric. Maybe if the community would cooperate with us we could clean up the hood—all hoods." His voice took on some heat.

"Trust takes two, Ortiz. Maybe if your brothers in blue stopped puttin' bullets in our backs we'd break bread with ya."

"I've never discharged my weapon let alone shoot—"

"And I'm about to email a video to a cop I just met so at least *we* are off to a good start," I say, noticing heat to my own voice. We sit silent a moment. His chest is probably rising and falling at the same high rate as mine.

"Thanks," he says, finally. "I'll check the video, and get back in a day or two. You get anything before that, let me know."

"Copy that." I'm about to click off.

"Moose."

"Yeah?"

"You better play me straight."

"This conversation's been had, Ortiz." I hang up.

I've been in this movie before. Every time I help people, and sometimes it dances around the edges of the law, sooner or later cops show up like sharks to chum'd waters. My mission is to help Alexandra, and my goal is to crush César's larynx. Now, with the cops involved, I'll have to play ball with them. Finesse is a must, moving forward.

I do a quick job of pouring alcohol on the knife wound and patch myself up. I should be excited about hitting the rack, but I always have trouble sleeping after fancy footwork with a cop. Interlacing my fingers behind my head, I stare at the ceiling far too long. Somewhere along the line, sleep comes.

❖ ❖ ❖

The slice to my arm isn't too bad. I change the bandage and get moving. Half an hour before visiting hours, I power up the F250 and point it toward the Silverlake Medical Center. My hope is that Alexandra will be up and around with her memory intact. César coming at me in my club raised the stakes like nobody's business. It also raises my commitment to seeing this thing through. I can't have someone on the streets gunning for me, period. He had his shot and missed, I won't.

Alexandra slow-smiles me when I walk in. Her eyes are clearer than before and carry a brightness that only adds to her natural beauty. If I weren't sortin' through her mess, I'd take my time and enjoy the vision. Her thick hair drapes over her shoulders and is brushed out like my first visit, only now it has a sheen to it. The bandage on her right arm has been changed and is much smaller. Her left shoulder is no longer in the temporary sling. She's a young woman on the mend, and I'm glad for it.

"Hello Moose, you didn't need to come back, honestly."

Were I another man perhaps I wouldn't.

"After what we been through, come on. I had to check on you."

"I hope to get out today," she says. "They haven't said when, just that the doctor needs to clear me."

I need to massage the conversation—play good cop a moment.

"Do ya mind?" I ask, sitting on the edge of the bed.

"Of course not," she says, pulling her legs up.

"Beautiful," I say motioning to the long-stem roses in the fake crystal vase at her bedside.

"Si," she says glancing. "Yellow are my favorite."

For a moment, she seems a trillion miles away from that night outside my crib. I ask her if the roses are from a family member. She tells me 'yes' but her body tenses slightly at the question. The Moose poking into family business is soon to be off-limits. I wait a beat.

"So, what's next for you? Some time off before headin' back to work? A little vacay maybe?"

"I'll take some time, yes," she says, hands clasped in her lap. "Look Moose, I want to thank you again for everything but—" She unclasps her hands and takes my big hard in both of hers. It's a gentle act, but the meaning is clear: thanks for the rescue now back away. I don't let her finish the goodbye speech.

"You know, I checked out César, the dude you mentioned."

Worry flashes across her face but she quickly tries to mask it.

"Yeah, I found a tag from one of the dogs and followed it up. Found the dog's original owner. Such a sweet 'ole lady, name was Georgia, no Graciella. Anyway, she made me these amazing homemade tamales. I can damn near taste 'em right now."

Alexandra shifts for comfort. I look to the ceiling, as if recalling the taste, but observe from the peripheral. She watches me.

"What's the hot tamale spot in town right now?" The question throws her.

"Oh, um Tres Tios, it's a food truck out of Long Beach. There's an app."

"Tres—ah, Three Uncles, gotta put that in my phone."

I take my time doing it. I want her to sweat a little. I can practically feel her discomfort. Generally, people don't like long silences.

I lower my voice and speak from my chest. "Who's César, Alexandra? I mean, who is he *really*?"

She can't hold my look. Her hands slip gently away and back to her lap. I give her more unsettling silence. She'll give, I just need to wait.

With a heavy sigh she opens up.

"César and I dated awhile."

"What's awhile?"

"We went out a couple of times."

"Keep goin'," I say.

"That's pretty much it. It wasn't that serious."

"He found me serious enough to come around to my job and make a play for me." My tone hardens more than I intend.

"Oh no."

"Look at my size. Now look into my eyes. D' ya think I'll take this shit lying down?"

Two tears escape the corners of her eyes. She wipes them away with the heel of her hand and struggles to hold it together. Part of me feels like a bully, but only the small part. The other part is tryin' to control my rage. César tried to kill both of us and now Alexandra's holding something back from me. I reach for the drink beside her bed and hand it to her. She takes it without comment and sips. I take the glass back, then trade it for a Kleenex box. She accepts this as well and mumbles a quiet thank you.

"You alright?"

She nods.

"Then go on, please. Leave nothin' out."

She stares at her fingers as she works at them, needlessly. "As I said, César and I went out a couple times but maybe, I don't know, I think he wanted more. I hadn't seen him for months, then out of the blue he calls me—all sweet on the phone and everything. That night he invited me out. Just to talk, he said. So, we talk. It was okay at first but then he starts talking crazy like we should be together. Why can't I give him a chance? This type of thing. Then—"

She locks up. The tears return. She grabs the Kleenex herself this time.

"Then?" I push.

"He tries to force himself on me. He pins me against the door and tries to kiss me. He was so strong there was little I could do. Next he went at *mi ropa.*

Her clothes. Shit.

"Fighting is no good, so I relax. He thinks I'm giving in, but I wait."

"For?"

"The right time."

"And then?" I ask, feeling my temperature rise.

"I strike him hard in his *juevos*—two times."

The fire I'd seen in her eyes that night on the blacktop rolls in like a tide.

"Then I jump out of the truck and run. I'm so upset and disoriented. He screams my name. I should have run to a house and asked for help, but I stayed on the street." She pauses and stares eyes unfocused at the room. "And then I hear the growling, and claws clicking fast on the street, and jingling chain sounds. "*Peros*," she whispers. "From hell."

She dabs tissue at her eyes. "Then I feel like a lightning bolt in the back of my leg. It feels like I've been shot by a bullet, but I know it is not. I hit the ground and—"

"I know the rest," I say. My jaw muscles clench. I look down and my fist is full of hospital bedding.

Alexandra takes a sip of the drink, then leans back heavily into the pillows. She's spent. I give her a moment but I'm not done. I notice the roses, the yellow ones she likes, need water. I fill the vase, then return it to the bedside table.

"Thanks for bein' truthful," I say.

She nods, ready to relax.

But I'm not done. "What do you do for work?"

"I work for a developer, an Asian guy. He's been in the news a couple times."

"He's not the one wantin' a run for Mayor is he? Donnie what'shisname?"

"Yes, that's him, Donnie Gan."

"Dude seems like a phony to me. Is he cool to work for?"

She works an answer around in her head and finally squeezes out, "He's fine."

I take a beat to process. I can tell my welcome is wearing thin.

"Last thing, then I'm on my way," I say cheerily. "Do you think César and Gan are connected in any way?"

Her soft browns widen to the size of quarters. Her response comes a little too quickly for my liking.

"Oh no. Mr. Gan? No, he'd never be involved with someone like César."

Then why would you? I want to ask but refrain.

"Please, Mr. Moose, I'd like to rest now. This is so upsetting."

"Of course. Just one—"

A male nurse enters the room. It's obvious he feels the room's energy is charged. He hesitates, looks at Alexandra briefly, before glaring at me. He's protective of the patient. The Moose has got no problem with that. I tell Alexandra I'll be in touch. She seems less than enthused about it.

◆ ◆ ◆

First thing I do when I get home is change into my gear and go to work on my heavy bag. It's one of my favorite ways to work out a problem. I normally go standard three-minute rounds and jump rope in between, but I haven't got that kind of time. Instead, I go hard for twenty minutes, non-stop. No breaks, not even for water. As a kid, I found an old bag in an abandoned building. I brought it home and strung it up. My grandma came barreling in, wanting to know what the racket was. I can almost remember the combination I was working on when she told me that if the bag helped stop the bullies in the hood from beatin' on me I could keep it. It's been part of my daily ever since.

❖ ❖ ❖

I show up for work early enough to handle the citrus and other chores. It's a wild night at the club, but not a particularly violent one. We have three bachelorette parties in at the same time. They go at it hard all night. Ninety minutes before closing, bachelorette party number one begins exotic dancing. As much as the security boys enjoy nights like these, they can be a serious pain in the ass. Hen party number two is in no mood to be outshined by the first party, so exposure ramps up. Naturally, bachelorette party number three weighs in.

"Jesus, Moose, I've never seen so many titties at once," Dave shouts.

"Too much info, bud. Go get that dancer off the table in section two. And double-time it 'cause that redhead from the other party is bee-lining hard for her."

"I see her. Shit, she got that look in her eye, too."

Dave takes off at a serious clip. I stay put, not wanting to leave my station unless it's serious. Dave manages to keep the ladies in check. The bachelorette parties continue their flare-ups for the entire shift. We don't toss them, because they drop righteous coin and boss Grimes likes it that way. Near the end of my shift, a woman who looks strangely familiar but out of place approaches. I keep her and Dave in my field of vision.

"Excuse me," she says, and hands me a business card. I turn it over and see that it's my own card.

"You're the Moose, right?" Her thick brown hair is almost black. She wears it down past the shoulder. The bottom three inches are dyed cherry red. Her faded black skinny jeans hug her shapely legs all the way south, where the bottoms stretch out to cover the tops of her black motorcycle boots. She wears a plain black t-shirt beneath a jean jacket, frayed at the bottom, where she's cut the seam off, making it cropped in style.

She wears little makeup but, in truth, doesn't need any. Her fit body reminds me of somebody else. There's an animal toughness to her eye that says to all predators, *you'll find no easy prey here*. She has an alertness I've seen in many high-level athletes, but there is something else, something harder I've seen only in ex-convicts.

She says hello and that her name is Jackie Lopez. A small, slightly calloused hand is offered. Her grip matches her hardness. Although her smile masks only part of her granite makeup, she's beautiful and very familiar. I place it as I release her hand.

"Doug "Moose" McCrae but e'body calls me Moose. I believe I know a relative of yours," I say.

"Yes, my sister Alexandra. You saved her life. I came to thank you."

I tell her she's welcome.

Tad, the bartender, slides down the bar and offers her a drink. She goes with a double Jameson, rocks. I study her as she orders—she knows I'm doing it. Tad moves back to his well and starts building. Jackie turns to me as she removes the jean jacket. Her sinewy arms are vascular, and although she doesn't have full sleeves, she has more tattoos than I can count.

I spy bouncer Dave and see his hands are full. Maybe I should assist, but this woman is a lead to my little project. Dave's dealt with worse. Tad places her drink on a plain black napkin and feeds her a corny smile. No doubt she and her sister experience that treatment often. She takes a decent pull then turns back to me.

"Join me?"

"Can't, on the clock."

She nods.

"I'm actually glad you're here, Jackie."

Her eyebrows rise with curiosity but it's an act. She knows what's coming.

"What can you tell me about César?" I ask.

"Oh, that asshole," she says, with a roll of her light brown eyes. "Alexandra dated him a couple of times—fuck knows why."

"He put them dogs on her," I say.

Rage flashes through her eyes like a slight disturbance to a curtain, then quickly subsides. Her lips become a straight line. It's the 'tell' of someone literally buttoning their lip.

"I can't buy she'd date a guy like that."

Her back straightens and her forearm muscles contract. Her eyes load with the ex-con anger I'd caught previously.

"You think you know my sister?"

The thickness of blood over water—sibling protectiveness…

"I get your point, but any man that would sic dogs on a woman, on anyone for that matter, would have a dozen tells as to what he is. Even on date number one it'd be broadcast like a billboard. I haven't known your sister long, but I know she's smarter than that."

Jackie gives me hard eyes. I have no problem with it, this is a hard business her sister's in. I push because it's been my experience that people talk under two circumstances; when drunk, or when angered. She downs the remainder of the Jameson and puts the glass down hard on the bar. Tad glances over but holds his position. If she decides to sock me in the mouth, I'll let her have one. She stares hard. Her taut body looks ready for action. She says nothing. Slowly, the rage drains from her eyes like the plug just got pulled from a tub full of water. She turns to Tad and taps her glass. Then back to me.

"I used to work nights. I bet you're wired after a shift."

"Can be," I tell her.

"And based on that big-ass build I bet you're hungry, too."

Flattery.

"Where you goin' with this, sister?"

The smile returns. "Let me take you out after your shift tonight as a thank you for helping Alexandra."

"You're on. Give me fifteen minutes."

She's moved off the César line of talk but I'm not worried. I plan on pressing it when we go out.

"Gives me time for this and maybe another," she says holding up her rock glass.

❖ ❖ ❖

I walk her to a sixties-era matte-black Ford Bronco II.

"You know Cut Brothers on La Brea?"

"Never been, but know it," I say.

"Good food and craft beers."

"Beer, at this hour? It's two-thirty a.m."

"If you know the password, there is."

I walk back to my truck and power up. Rolling away from the club, we have to take a right onto La Brea. Jackie eases into traffic.

I'm forced to wait for two cars to pass before my turn. To my left, a classic Chevy Impala barrels past. Probably a drunk driver. He won't get ten blocks at this time of night without landing a DUI. He cuts off a late-model Camry, squeezes in behind Jackie and hugs her bumper like a spider monkey. I don't like it. I pin my accelerator and move over one lane, hovering near the Impala's back quarter panel. I make out two people, driver and passenger, no one in back. I've seen all I need to see.

A block and a half rolls by. Cut Brothers comes up on our right but Jackie blows by without slowing. Clever, she knows she's pulling a tail. I move up level with her. Our eyes lock. With quick hand gestures I tell her to take the next right then drive slow. She nods. We both know this is related to the dog attack. I push ahead and take a right— one block past her block—and parallel her one block over.

I'm familiar with the residential streets, which are controlled by four-way stops. It takes me three blocks to get ahead of the two-car convoy. I punch it and clear two more blocks, then take a hard right down a narrow street. Apartment buildings fill both sides of the street and few of them have underground parking. This means parked cars are on both sides, which makes a tight fit for the King Ranch. I don't care. I hit the switch that brings in the side mirrors, and hammer the gas pedal. The end of the block is coming up. Jackie's Bronco II stops at the sign, then rolls through the intersection. The Impala sticks to her without stopping. My truck is outfitted with police-issue black-steel push bars on the front bumper. I'm gonna to use 'em.

Both driver and passenger stare straight ahead, confident the big truck to the left will hold at the stop sign. I bury the pedal and T-bone the Impala center-mass of the driver door. Front and rear wheels on the driver's side leave the pavement. The car skids sideways for twelve feet before gravity brings the car back to the pavement.

I make a hard left, then crank right down an alley, and slam the truck in park. I sprint back to the Impala toward the passenger door. The driver will be out cold or at least a minor threat. I haul open the passenger door and yank a slender, light-skinned brother out. He goes for his waistband. I pin his hand there, then give him a stiff palm to the eye socket with my free hand. His legs go wobbly, but I hold him and relieve him of his .45-caliber Beretta. Using my loud voice for the benefit of any onlookers, I ask, "Hey bud, are you okay?" Then, leaning in close I whisper, "Nod if you work for César."

"Dude that hurt, I ain't tellin' you—"

With my thumb and third finger I grab him by the sternocleidomastoid muscle, the muscle that turns your neck left and right. I squeeze like juicing a lemon. He winces and grabs at my hand. The pain hits the pressure point while sending shooting pain to the temple. It also gives the feeling of choking.

"I said, nod for César. Headshake for no."

His face reddens and sweat gathers on his forehead. He manages a slight nod.

"Tell him the guy that killed his dogs says nowhere is safe. And the name's Moose." I draw my hand back to put him to sleep when Jackie gently grabs my shoulder.

"Please Moose, let me," she says. I still have him by the neck muscle but move to the side.

With eyes empty of emotion, she draws her leg back and kicks him square in the nuts with her steel-toed motorcycle boot.

"That's if you ever try to follow me again," she says, before spitting on him. "*Puta!*"

He passes out. When he wakes, his nuts will be the size of cantaloupes. I let him drop, then peek in at the driver. He's still out cold. Onlookers begin creeping out of shadows and onto stoops. I pull the magazine from his gun, along with the bullet in the chamber, wipe the piece down, then toss it onto the floor in the back.

"Stay here, bud, we goin' for help," I say loudly, grabbing Jackie by the arm and moving her down the block. We get to the mouth of the alley.

"Thanks, Moose."

"Don't mention it."

"Can we take a rain check on Cut Brothers?" She rolls her neck, cracking it. "I feel kinda—"

"No sweat, but I'm gonna need to talk to you and your sister."

"Couple of days?"

"Tomorrow," I say, and head to my truck. Halfway down the alley, I call the law. I report the accident and that the occupants were waving guns around at bystanders. I hang up, and three blocks later a symphony of sirens hits my ears. Serve and protect team inbound.

❖ ❖ ❖

The Lopez sisters rent a two bedroom, one-and-a-half bath bungalow on Sanborn Street near Sunset Boulevard. The tiny lawn out front is the same burnt brown color as mine. Most of us haven't watered our lawns in months since the governor announced we're all drying up together.

If the house is over a thousand square feet it can't be by much. The canary yellow paint job with white trim will need a touch-up next year. Jackie's Bronco is parked out front. A mid-2000 gray

Honda Civic is parked behind it. I wonder if it's Alexandra's.

At the front door, a black security door bars entry. It opens as I'm about to knock.

"Alexandra, you lookin' good." And she does. She's healing fast—must be youth and good genes.

"Please come in."

The door opens directly into a living room. A large leather sectional faces a sixty-inch TV. The rectangular glass-top coffee table is too small for the couch. It holds a *Shape Magazine* and three remotes. Alexandra forces a pleasant smile as I enter. Jackie comes from the tiny galley kitchen and we get down with the pleasantries. But it's awkward, so I pick an antique wing without being offered, and sit.

"So, César, let's get into it." I turn serious. "We got the attempted murder by pits, attempted fuck-knows-what on Jackie by two fools that work for César, and an attack on me."

"You?" Jackie asks.

"César came at me with a blade. Made a play at my club." I sit forward on my seat and rest my elbows on my knees.

"All that being said, I'm going to wipe César off the chessboard."

Alexandra looks tentative. Jackie bites her bottom lip and nods.

"Good. The dogs that attacked you, Alexandra, were no ordinary dogs. Someone, I'm guessing César, turned them mean and has been using them for fighting. It was my suspicion that night outside my place, and it's been confirmed by a cop on the scene."

They exchange quick looks at the mention of police.

"This cop has taken more than a mild interest in me, which pushes my clock. So, here's my question: Where does César hold these fights?"

43

The sisters move close to one other and speak in hurried Spanish. Even with my little understanding, it's obvious they're deciding how much to tell me.

"Spill it girls. I know you didn't ask for my help, but I'm in it now. César coming at me seals it. Time and place. Now."

"Okay, okay," Alexandra says. "It's true, the dogs fight at a place near Agoura Hills."

"Either of you ever witness the fights?"

"I have," Alexandra says. "One time. I nearly got sick."

"Pinpoint it on your phone and forward it to me. Now, please."

She seems on autopilot as she works a map app. Jackie waits patiently, looking at me with a look that gives nothing. The message comes through. I glance at it, widen the screen, then close my phone.

"Any idea when the next fight might be?" I know the question is a long shot.

"Tonight, midnight."

The corner of my mouth goes up in a half grin.

❖ ❖ ❖

I formulate a plan as the day presses on. My first stop is Silva's Camera Shop in East Hollywood. I speak to the short jovial clerk in round specs with male pattern baldness.

"What can we do for you today?"

"I called earlier about renting a camera, something suitable for a night shoot."

"McCrae right? It was me you hollered at on the phone. Geez, you're a big fella," he says with a polite laugh. I don't respond.

"Follow me," he says with an exaggerated wave of his skinny arm.

I follow him down the long glass-top counter until he stops and bends down. He comes up with a camera and places it on the glass. "The Cannon EDS 80. This bad boy retails for just over a thousand bucks, rents for one-o-five per day. Now, obviously we have higher-end stuff here, but you mentioned you're out to capture the moon, yes?"

"That's right, always been a moon guy."

"Right. This baby will be fine but—" he says, holding up his pointer finger, "I'm gonna set you up with a more powerful lens."

"Now we're talkin'." I shoot him my best Moose grin.

We walk another three steps down the counter. He squats down and digs around, then comes up with a lens nearly the length of my forearm. He removes the stock lens and attaches the larger one, then leans both elbows on the glass and gives me a tour of the camera.

I'm interested but there's a but... "I'll be straight with ya, sir, this outfit is perfect for my moon project but I'm on a nightclub bouncer's salary. You got any wiggle room on that rental price?"

He pushes his glasses up his nose and studies me a moment.

"It's too bad you didn't come in yesterday, we had a twenty-percent off discount."

"Really? Shame. One photog' to another, the moon wasn't full yesterday."

A grin spreads slowly over his face. "Good point and even better bargaining skills. I'll give you the twenty off." He caps that statement with the polite laugh, again.

"Good lookin' out, brother."

I sign on the dotted line, leave the credit card deposit, and head home to plot where I'm going for grub. I'll need to eat before tonight's outing and don't feel like heating up leftovers. A few street tacos might hit the spot. Fernando's Tacos is one of my top three favorite taco trucks. All I need to do is find it.

Back in the F250, I open the app. The food truck is mere blocks from my house. I know the area. It's a new condo complex under construction. It's two forty-five in the p.m. right now, which means the truck is at the site for the construction crew's three p.m. coffee break. I can have my tacos in ten minutes; timing couldn't be more perfect.

❖ ❖ ❖

At the kitchen table, I check the lay of the land on my laptop. The dog-fight property in Agoura Hills has a semi-ranch style set-up. Most of the terrain is dry grass and dirt. A street named Honeysuckle parallels the 101 Freeway, and from there, a two-mile dirt road serves as a driveway up to the ranch. Paths spike off from the long drive in various directions. Some seem wide enough for dirt bike paths while others look like little fingerlings made for hiking.

There are three buildings in total on the property and a long path at the end of the driveway leads to the main building. Directly in front is a large circular area. I zoom in on the map. Looks like a makeshift amphitheater. This must be where the sadistic battles take place.

Directly behind the main building sits a smaller structure, might even be a motorhome. About a quarter mile to the northeast of the amphitheater is the smallest of the three buildings. It's difficult to read any details of what it might be, a shed maybe. Either way, that's my destination. I'll hole up there and see what I can through the high-powered telephoto.

My pack is nearly full when I reach for my gun. It doesn't need checking, but I need to do something while weighing my options. I eject the magazine and check the 115-grain bullets. If I have any run-in with the cops it won't go well for me dressed as I am, along with my size and skin color. With a sigh, I push the fifteen-round magazine back into the frame and put the gun back. The plan is for long-distance surveillance, nothing up close. *The gun won't be necessary*, I tell myself.

I hop on the 101 Freeway, which has various designations depending where you drive on it. Where I get on, it's called the Hollywood Freeway. As it moves into Ventura County it becomes the Ventura Freeway, and so on, all the way up to the Golden Gate Bridge in San Francisco where it becomes the Redwood Highway. For ease of conversation, everyone calls her the 101, plain and simple.

Traffic is light. I make my exit, and cross through the major intersection, make a right on Honeysuckle. From there I find the gas station and pull into a spot beside the air and water machine. This gives a direct sight line to the ranch driveway through my high-powered lens. I lift the lens only when the coast is clear of patrons moving from their cars into the store. I don't want to attract any attention during this age of 'see something, say something.'

At eleven-twenty p.m. two vehicles practically piggyback down the driveway. One is a late-model Land Rover Discovery and the other is a limousine. Another five minutes pass. Then, several cars enter the driveway in a convoy. Each vehicle is visible for about eight seconds before the brake lights are swallowed by dust and darkness. By eleven-forty more cars arrive. That's my cue. Time for a hike. The pack jingles quietly as I put it on. I take it off again, find the loose zipper and duct tape it silent.

"Move yo' ass, Moose," I say.

The trail is an easy, solid gravel trek that winds left and right but generally heads southwesterly. I reach a copse of oak trees and emerge out the other side—to find I'm standing on charred ground—a victim of one of Southern California's many forest fires. Traffic noise sounds like a distant ocean, and over it is the sound of people cheering and dogs barking. The sound is disorienting at first, as the noise bounces and ricochets off the trees. I work through the trees until I find the smallest of the three structures I'd seen on the map.

The full moonlight shines down on a planked structure close to thirty feet long, all one level. An eight-foot tall aluminum ladder is embedded on the outside, giving access to the roof. There's a lot of barking coming from the inside. I lean my back against the planks and peek around the corner. The structure is a dog kennel, and a large pit bull in the first cage leaps at the chain-link fencing. The dogs seem irritated by my presence, but also fired up by the sounds coming from the amphitheater, below. Not wanting to draw the attention of a sentry, if there is one, I move to the back of the kennel and down the building.

At the opposite end, I discover a guard leaning against the wall, staring at his phone. He's wearing a Colt model AR-15 with a sixteen-inch barrel strapped across his chest. I'm lucky he hasn't seen me. Yet. I creep twenty yards away from the kennel and find a eucalyptus tree easy enough to climb. Once settled, I zero the long camera lens in on the fights.

My hunch was right. The circle is a sunken amphitheater. About seventy people sit and watch the carnage in the center of a caged-in area. I lower the camera the moment a pit bull gets a rottweiler by the throat and is about to finish it off. My teeth grit and my jaw clenches. I want to kill César in that moment. I shake it off and raise the lens.

The victor is gone from the cage. Two men drag the fallen dog by the hind legs. I sweep the camera and take in more visual. Heavily armed men in groups of two move through the crowd and collect cash and take bets. Then they move to a man seated at small folding table. He's bookended by two guards. There's a money counter on the table. Money comes to him, gets counted, then two separate guards move the cash to the rear tent. The flap is barely open enough for me to see the cash get dropped off at the limousine.

I move over the crowd and look for César and notice each attendant wears a lanyard around their neck with a laminate at the bottom. I sharpen the image and click off a few pics of the laminate. I continue clicking photos of guests.

Finally, I find César. Two security guards stand behind him as he speaks to a short Asian man in a high-dollar, tailored suit. I snap away, this guy has the look of importance. When I adjust focus, I nearly drop the camera. The man is Donnie Gan, big-time real estate developer, wannabe politician and Alexandra's boss.

"Mutha fu—"

I hear a voice from the kennel call, "Jimmy." Somebody's coming.

Time to go.

I dismantle the camera as quickly and quietly as I can and put it back in the pack. I slide the pack back on and silently ease down the tree. The guards are swapping positions. I hide behind the tree and realize I should have picked a thicker tree. Standing sideways, I suck in my gut and hold my breath.

"Keep an eye out," the second guard says. "Something or somebody's got Gan spooked. No surprises, somebody might be up here. I need this job."

"Copy that, Lyle," Jimmy says.

Confirmed: Gan runs the show.

I let my breath out slowly as footsteps near. I crouch low, banking that most people don't look down. Jimmy's headed my way down toward the amphitheater. A second later he's right on top of me. I come up fast and lift the barrel of the AR with me. Three rounds pop off in under a second. Damn, that only happens if the safety's off, with your finger resting on the trigger. He struggles to pull the gun from me. I use his momentum and force the butt of the weapon up under his chin. His head rocks back. With a better grip on the gun than he has, I hit him square in the nose.

Jimmy the sentry is out cold. I let him drop and toss his weapon. His buddy calls to him from the kennel. I consider hanging around and taking out the second guard, but with shots fired, the element of surprise is gone… not to mention I'm sure reinforcements are on the way. I take off running. I'm fast for a big man but have no desire to sprint all the way back to the truck. My hope is that he'll give up the chase. As a bouncer, I rarely go off the reservation to break up a fight. I hope Gan hands down the same policy to his staff.

I make great time through the oaks and double-time it once I reach the scorched earth. Occasionally, I zig and zag in the event a guard comes out of the trees and blazes away. I half expect a bullet in the back, but am grateful to make it to the second stand of trees. My wind is holding up so I maintain my pace, although cautiously, not wanting to roll an ankle and go ass over teakettle down the final slope.

Finally, I hop in my truck, fire it up and spit gravel as I gun-it in reverse.

※ ※ ※

I hold the truck under the speed limit on the way home. The final ounce of adrenaline finally works its way out of my system, and I feel relaxed and satisfied. I use the drive to put together what I know: Donnie Gan is in charge and César is his trigger-man, using dogs as his weapon of choice—not counting the knife he used on me. Was César acting alone when he went after Alexandra, or was he following orders? It's one of the many questions I need an answer for and mean to get it.

If the public finds out about Gan's involvement in dog fights, his political aspirations will be done. He'll do jail time. I could hand César over to Officer Ortiz and he'd do time, too, for the dogs. And chances are he's got other warrants out, waiting for him. Tossing him to the cops is the right play, but before I do that I'll need to hurt him first—physically.

My truck rumbles onto the bumpy lane dividers. I'm thinking too deeply. I correct the path and move on to the Lopez sisters. Alexandra lied about César and Gan being connected—why? And why lie to the Moose who's helping you? More questions. But it's always like this when I try to help people with a mess: a pile of questions, a fixated forward-moving Moose, then the solution. Still, being lied to pisses me off. But I know liars. They lie out of fear, greed or both. Find out what scares them or financially motivates, and truth is what's left.

※ ※ ※

The next morning, I show up at the Lopez sisters' home unannounced.

I take the camera off my shoulder and pull up the pics from last night.

"Peep this right here."

Their expressions are the same, as their heads touch, staring into the tiny camera window. I was careful to put Donnie Gan's pictures at the end. It registers more on Alexandra's face than her sister's. It's the look of the guilty.

"Look, Moose, I know I said that my boss and César weren't—"

"Sixty seconds," I say.

"Huh?"

"Sixty... seconds," I repeat with heat.

"I don't like your tone, Moose," Jackie says, stepping in front of her sister.

"That's how long you had, sixty seconds tops, and those dogs would have gotten to your carotid and ripped your throat out. Then, as you bled out, they'd have eaten you alive and for a moment you'd be aware o' that shit."

"Hey, lay off!" Jackie shouts.

Alexandra fights back tears.

"If I hadn't come out of my house, hadn't 'made the *choice*...'" I pause, and only our breathing can be heard. "You'd be without a sister, Jackie."

"We said 'thank you,'" Jackie says through gritted teeth.

"We didn't ask you to get involved," Alexandra says. I wait a beat. I want the silence to make them feel uncomfortable.

"Uh-huh you thanked me, and I said you're welcome. You didn't ask for my help but that ain't up to you. But what is gospel is that lying to me is about the dumbest thing y'all could do. César, or for all we know, Donnie Gan, has taken runs at all three of us. You girls should be making my job easier instead o' play actin' like a couple high-school gossip queens." I practically shout the last sentence. The room goes quiet again until the silence is broken by the beeping of a coffee maker. The girls ignore it at first.

Finally... "Coffee?" Alexandra asks solemnly.

"Why the hell not?" I say, and sit down heavily.

We fix the coffees, then get into it. The girls apologize for bullshitting me and promise it won't happen again. My grandmother used to say 'promises bring comfort to fools.' Alexandra holds the floor. She tells me what it's been like working for Gan and that she actually knew César more than she'd originally told me, but that the story of him forcing himself on her was bogus.

"Truth is, he offered me a ride home but didn't talk at all. He just stared out the window. The vibe was off. I knew something was up, but we were heading toward my home so I wasn't too worried. Then—" she paused and worked at her cuticles.

"And then?" I push.

"He says, 'get out.' So I do, but then he got out, too. When I saw he was going to the back of the truck I knew why he was acting so weird. I've never run so fast in my whole life."

"Have any idea why he was trying to kill you with the dogs?"

She hangs her head. "Thirty thousand dollars."

"What?" That makes me sit straight up.

"That's how much I owe Donnie Gan. Thirty K. I borrowed it."

I let a heavy wind blow out of my lips. These things always involve money.

"Why would you need that kind of dough?" I watch her but spy on Jackie out of the corner of my eye. Alexandra looks up from her lap and shoots a quick glance at her sister. The look says either she's about to confess something to the new stranger among them or that Jackie better back the lie that's coming.

"It's for our mother. She's, well, not legal, and we want to bring her here. Jackie and I were born here. We're citizens but our mother is not."

I look to Jackie to see if her eyes verify, and without a hiccup, she takes over.

"And immigration has been so tough with this current asshole president. We've lined up a coyote to bring her over the Texas border. That's why Alexandra borrowed the money."

I let it roll around in my head. If true, then Gan would want to see his money, which would mean he wouldn't have made the kill order. That meant César acted on his own. Why? Questions.

"I'm sorry we didn't tell you." Alexandra takes over. "But hiring coyotes and talking smuggling isn't the kind of news we share with a stranger." She hesitates. "Even if the stranger is a good man, which you are. But this is family."

The story adds, but it came out at bullet-train speed, which is a little too quick for my liking.

"Did Gan say when you gotta pay him back?"

"No."

"He puttiin' interest on that?"

"No."

I don't like that. It doesn't smell right. I ask a few more questions about Gan but don't get much.

❖ ❖ ❖

I already have Donnie Gan's address from before I met with the sisters. I'm going with or without their blessing. Back on the 101, heading north, I get to Gan's city of Woodland Hills in forty-five minutes. A wrought-iron gate protects the driveway with a yin and yang medallion at the center. Sitting atop white concrete pillars are samurai soldiers. I park outside and buzz the panel beside the gate. When I announce my name, a voice comes out of an aluminum box asking if I have an appointment.

"No, but it's 'bout César, and Mr. Gan will want to hear this," I say.

A massive security guard of Samoan descent emerges from my left. When I lean into the gate, I see the guard shack he perches in.

"What about César?" the guard, built like a sumo wrestler, asks.

"For Gan's ears only, bud, let's go."

He gives a high-pitch giggle with a smile that spreads the length of the Grand Canyon across his face. "If you ever do stand-up comedy let me know, I'll come check you out."

"Open up, bud," I say.

"Not gonna happen."

"Suppose I have info that César is sleepin' with Gan's partner, or that he's been talking to the cops about his shady stuff, or that he's been skimming off the dog fights."

The big guard's smile slides away.

"That's right, just open up, save your job."

He reaches into the breast pocket of his blazer, pulls a remote and opens the gate.

He steps close to me to show that, as big as I am, he's bigger. He's an inch and a half taller, three inches wider and fifty pounds heavier. I played against guys his size and was his equal in weight a lifetime ago. His intent to intimidate me falls pancake flat.

"Follow me, tough guy," he says, down to me.

"Thought you'd never ask."

We walk up the brown slate drive. Two black Bentleys and a Range Rover are parked side by side at forty-five degree angles to the massive wooden front door. My Samoan escort hands me off to another guard whose size is closer to mine. The Samoan gives him the abridged version of who I am. Guard number two grabs my arm at the elbow and attempts to guide me.

"That's a mistake," I say, and shake him loose.

The big Samoan giggles, "He's not your type, Steve, just get him to Gan. But if he acts up, please hit me up on the radio. I'd love to teach him some manners."

"Okay, Fetu, you got it," my new friend says and gives me a hand palm-up, indicating me to go first and lead the way. Our route, once inside, is a straight shot. We walk through a large, empty, white-tiled foyer, past a seating area that looks unused, down a wide hallway with white walls devoid of any artwork and through modern folding accordion doors to a pool area, outside. On the far side of the pool is a covered cabana with a man sitting on a chaise lounge.

My escort calls across the pool,

"He says he has news on César."

"Bring him over," Donnie Gan calls back, with a bored wave of the hand.

My friend shoves me in the back.

"Mistake number two," I say. "Now there's gonna be payment."

"Move it, tough guy," he says. 'Tough Guy' must be in the Gan employee handbook of phrases. We walk around the large rectangle pool and stand over Donnie Gan. He blocks the sun with his hand. He's skinnier than in photos. His goatee is thinner than a twelve-year old boy's. He has the kind of eyes that make you want to check your pockets. Slippery isn't slippery enough a word for him. His bony chin juts out in full arrogance. His voice is deeper than I expect. It's obviously practiced.

"Wow, you're as big as my security. You looking for a job? You want to take César's place? What's his name, Steve?"

My escort's face flushes.

"He didn't ask, but the name's Moose."

"Moose? Like the animal?"

"Exactly. I'm here to talk about dogs, fighting dogs."

He sits up and puts a leg on either side of the chaise.

"What the fuck do you want?"

"Huh, y'all were so polite three seconds ago," I say.

"Make your point."

Steve steps closer.

"Move back, Steve, or I'll break you and I ain't talkin' hurt feelings," I say, without giving him so much as a glance.

"Boss?" he asks. Gan raises a palm, holding him back.

"I'm here about yo' assistant, Alexandra. Dogs, four of them, attacked her. She survived, but you already know that."

"So, tell me what I don't know, Mr. Moose, or was it Mouse?"

"Comedy ain't your thing, Gan. Like I say, she was attacked. I bring it up and ya don't seem to give a damn."

He sips his cocktail and says nothing.

"She borrowed money from ya and she intends to pay ya back, so why the dog attack?"

Donnie gets up from his chaise. Steve inches forward. I shoot him a look, which freezes him where he stands.

"Mr. Mouse, I'm sorry, Moose, my employee borrowed this money, yes. So, if I send dogs I don't get money. Why do that? I love money. Conversation, discussion, and pow-wow is now over. Steve, show him the door." He waves his hand and sits back down.

Steve comes in fast and reaches for me. I put up my hands as though I don't want any trouble, then send a hard right to his solar plexus. He goes down wheezing and takes a knee. I turn to Gan.

"Here or the pool, Gan?" I say.

"You're the Moose, you choose," he says with exaggerated boredom.

I put a hard knee to Steve's ribs and send him into the pool.

"Let's say, hypothetically, I know of dog fights. And let's say last night somebody came snooping around and concussed one of my security guards." He steps within an inch of me—and of his life—if I want it to go that way.

"You know anything about this incident?"

"Hypotheticals are time wasters, Gan," I say, looking down on him. He backs up three steps. Steve crawls out of the pool and struggles to hands and knees. He tries to get his feet under him but it's no good. He's starts coughing and spitting up pool water.

"I told you there'd be payment, Steve," I tell him.

He looks to Gan, who tells him to go get cleaned up and think hard about his future. The scolding done, he turns to me.

"If you're going to be in the business of fix and rescue, you need to know your client. Really know them. You ask the wrong questions, Mr. Moose."

I don't say anything.

"Ah, I see your mind is working. Maybe you're more than just three hundred pounds of muscle."

"Two-sixty," I say. "What do you mean 'know my client'?"

"Tell Alexandra I have it all on tape. You won't understand that, but she will." He sips his drink. "Now get the fuck off my property or I'll call Fetu. He's not like Steve."

"Fetu'd take some work but the result would be the same."

I got all I was going to get and it was more than enough for me. Just one more thing.

"You gonna run for mayor, Gan?" I ask.

"Maybe yes, maybe no."

"That means yes. I'm gonna go to Vegas and bet heavily against ya. Have a nice day."

I leave the same way I entered. Fetu is waiting for me at the gate.

"I never got the call, so I guess today you live."

"I'll tell ya the same thing I told Gan, comedy ain't fo' you. Now open that gate before ya regret taking this job."

He gives me the same giggle he had earlier and lets me out. We'll meet again, I'm sure of it.

❖ ❖ ❖

I'd been blindsided by the sisters again, and barely five minutes after reading them the riot act. Too much smoke and too many mirrors with those two. I get part way into dialing their number but click off. I'll deal with the sisters later. Coming at them now just gives them time to cook up the next story.

I get home, pull out the violin. Only I don't play it, I clean it instead. It really doesn't need it but the ritual relaxes me. Once clean, I lay it on my coffee table underneath the skylight so the light catches it just right. I don't leave it there long, since the sun's not good for it. But just for a moment so she can glisten and I can admire the craftsmanship.

My stomach growls. I don't have proper dinner grub but there are cold cuts, cheeses and crackers in the fridge. I'm ready to tear into a giant one-man platter when there's a knock at the door.

"Alexandra," I say, with the door open.

"Sorry for just showing up. Are you busy?" She attempts to peek around me. She looks distraught.

"Nah, come in. What's got you rattled?"

"I'm in way over my head, Moose. I don't know what to—I'm so scared," she says, and practically lunges for me, throwing her arms around my waist and burying her head in my chest. I put an arm around her and hold her close. Her hug tightens as she begins to sob.

"It's all right," I say, inhaling the sweet lemony fragrance of her thick hair. "We got this."

"I'm freaking out," she says. I gently pull her away from me. Her soft brown eyes begin to fill with water.

"What happened?"

"I got a call from Jerry, he's a sort of an errand boy for Gan. He's pretty much the only person I trust over there."

"What'd he say?" "He says Gan's entire place is wired for surveillance, every room. I knew he had security cameras, but Jerry said everywhere and—"

"What did you do?" I ask, putting a hand on each of her toned shoulders. "What did Gan see?"

Her shoulders drop with a heavy sigh.

"I saw an email on his laptop, one I wasn't supposed to see."

"Can't you say it was an accident?"

"I printed it out," she says, which brings more tears.

We face each other without words. That explains Gan's 'I got everything on tape' comment. This stunt of hers may have been a bridge too far for Gan.

"This Jerry dude, he say anything else?"

She closes her eyes a moment, thinking back, then says, "What the hell am I doing? I have it here." She digs out her phone, puts the message on speaker.

"He knows, Alexandra. Gan knows. This place is wired, every room. He said something about an email. Shit, what did you do? Actually, don't tell me. And don't come back here, get out now. I gotta go. Be safe.

I replay the tape in case I missed anything.

"The brother's stressed," I say.

She nods.

"When ya get this?"

"It came in Saturday... the day of the attack. Only I just—"

She locks up, runs a hand through her hair, then buries her face in her hands.

"You just picked up the message today," I say finishing the sentence for her.

"Looks like Gan put César onto you regardless of the thirty large—fingers point his way." I pause.

"What? What is that look on your face, Moose?"

"You better show me that email."

I expect her to pull it up on her phone or tell me she'll email it later. Instead, she reaches into her back pocket and hands me a single piece of paper.

"You planned on showing me this today."

"Yes."

I take it to my couch and sit. She joins me.

To: L. Chenowith

From: D. Gan

In regards to my rental properties I was wondering if there is a legal procedure that can filter my applicants in such a way that I can avoid renting to a certain ethnicity? Specifically is there a method I could employ to avoid renting units to African American tenants? I feel this is a profitable policy and am committed on this. Your immediate attention is appreciated.

Regards,

Donnie

"Chenowith is his lawyer?"

"Yes."

"What kinda fool puts his racist shit in writing?" I say, not looking for a response. "Can I keep this?"

"I made it for you."

"By giving me this you must want something."

"I do, I want you to keep going even if something happens to me or Jackie."

"The only thing that's gonna happen is we win this thing. This email seals it."

"You have a plan?"

"Damn near," I tell her.

She gets up and paces in front of me. The tears are gone and the determined face I'd seen fighting the dogs peers down at me.

"I want this to end."

"Working on it."

"Not just César and Gan, or my situation, I'm talking about all of the Gans out there. The greedy 'money means everything' crowd, the racist pigs that lock immigrant kids in cages and the *cabrones* that lock black people out of apartments. I'm sick of it," she says pointing at me. "Jackie and I, we are survivors, we've battled monsters before. Whatever your plan is," she says lowering her voice and locking eyes with me, "We are in. All the way."

And then she grabs each of us a beer, and I settle back as Alexandra unloads and tells me what César really does for Gan…

César is the last one of his three-man crew to step out of the 1977 deep-purple sparkle Chevy Impala. He slams the door closed, then checks his look in the window's reflection. His hair is slicked back and held down by a black hair net. He always does this when he wears his number-one beige fedora with the black and white hatband. The top button of his black-and-white checked, long sleeve shirt is done up. The white t-shirt beneath is spotless. His thin mustache is on point. He adds a slight tilt to the fedora. This makes him smile.

His baggy beige khakis go all the way down to his white-soled black runners. He doesn't wear his khakis short and below the knee like his boys, Rocco and Gordo. He's got no problem with the long, white, tube sock and runners look, he just prefers the full-length pant. He turns and smiles at Rocco, the Hispanic-Black mixed henchman. Rocco's had to prove himself more than anyone else, being that his father is black—and he has many times over. César trusts him like a brother and never doubts his loyalty to him or their gang Perros de Guerra. And that's what they are: dogs of war ready to throw down with anybody, at any moment, who impedes their interests.

Gordo, the fat one, barely says two words per day. He's a loyal bastardo, too. This is why they are often César's top choice for runs big or small.

Today's run is minor, a walk in the park, which is why César leaves his Smith and Wesson 40 Shield under the front seat of the car.

"Let's go bitches," César says, leading the way, as always, through the parking lot toward the neighborhood grocery mart door. Rocco and Gordo scan the surroundings. They both have snub-nose 38's tucked into waistbands under their white t's. They're strapped for whatever comes their way. César, not wanting to be picked up with a piece on him should the cops roll up, only carries when the gig is hot.

The electronic bell chimes as César enters. "Chill," he says to the pimply-faced store clerk with nervous eyes. "We're not here to rob you, not today, anyway."

Rocco laughs. The trio marches down three separate aisles. At the back of the store they find the elderly black woman they're looking for.

"Ms. Emery," César says, with a car salesman smile.

"Yes?"

César can tell she's scared. He ramps up the intimidation by rattling off her address.

"What the hell you want?" she responds. César knows she's trying her best to show some backbone but it isn't working.

"You got ten days to vacate your apartment."

Her expression moves from fear to anger.

"You think I don't know who you work for? I pays my rent," she says, gripping her basket firmly and stiffening her posture. César hauls out his phone and pulls up a picture of a little girl. He holds the phone sideways, for Ms. Emery to see.

"I believe your granddaughter's name is Aisha. Looks like she's having fun in the park, doesn't it?"

Ms. Emery starts to tremble. It's the effect César is looking for.

"You touch her and I'll kill you," she warns.

"Ten days and I won't have to touch her. Don't do as I say and little Aisha will never play again."

The elderly woman continues to shake. César can feel the rage coming off her. He peeks at the groceries in her basket.

"Hmm, I think twenty bucks ought to cover your shit," he says pulling a twenty off his thick wad of bills and dropping it into the basket.

"Ten days, woman."

"Screw you!"

César's crew vacates. They hop into the Impala. César turns the engine over and revs it twice, then hits the hydraulic lift button. The front-end rises up, followed by the back. Then he eases it down and drives out of the lot.

65

"We got one more stop, cabrones," he says.

"Let's do it," Rocco says. *"Then we can blaze."*

"You know it," César says. *"Hey, Gordo."* He checks Gordo in the rearview. Gordo catches his look with bored eyes.

"You gonna talk today or wait until tomorrow?" Both he and Rocco laugh. After a beat Gordo says, *"No se."*

César and Rocco crack up even harder.

"Ya hear that, Rocco? That fool say he ain't sure if he gonna talk today. That's fucked up."

Gordo turns his head and gazes out the window. After the laughter dies, Rocco asks who the last client is and makes air quotes with his hands around the word client.

"We got Beaman."

"That old fuck. Easy day, huh fools?"

"Yeah, nigga."

Five minutes later they pull up to Hobart Beaman's apartment building. As they walk through the courtyard, doors close and curtains are pulled over windows. César loves the fear he instills in people. They vault the stairs at the rear of the complex and pound on Mr. Beaman's security door. His inner door is open.

"I ain't buyin' shit. Go 'way." His raspy voice comes from inside.

"Open up, Beaman, it's César."

"César? You tell that Chinese muthafucka Gan that my rent's paid."

"Change in plans, homie, we need your place."

"Let me be one of many on this fine muthafuckin' day to tell y'all greasy bitches to go fuck yo' selves."

"That's not nice, Mr. Beaman," César says fumbling with a set of master keys.

"I hear you been runnin' folks outta they places but ya ain't runnin' me no place. Dis nigga stayin' put."

César finds the key and puts it in the lock.

"Don't you come up in here. I got my Mossberg across my lap."

César struggles with the rusty lock by jiggling the key. "Oh really? Let me hear you rack that shit then. I think you bluffin'."

He signals the boys to get their pieces out, then finally gets the door unlocked. César listens another moment but hears no shotgun racking. He slips into the apartment. Mr. Beaman sits at a tiny kitchen table. Two of the wooden table legs are held together with duct tape. A half-eaten breakfast of bacon, eggs and toast sits on a plate in front of the aging black man. Rocco and Gordo move quickly and haul him to the floor.

"You think you can threaten with a shotgun you don't even have, asshole?" Rocco says, putting a knee across his chest.

"Get the fuck off me, man," Beaman says.

Rocco punches him hard in the face. The old man shakes it off and glares at Rocco.

"Got some fight left in you, old man, I'll give you that." César sits at the old man's breakfast and digs into it. "Gordo, check the place and make sure nobody else is here."

"I got yo' mamma in the back bedroom sleeping off the sex I gave her," Beaman says. Rocco hits him again.

"Hobart Beaman we're going to relieve you of this apartment."

"When I was your age I coulda kicked the shit out o' all three of yuz. But y'all come in here with guns and eat another man's breakfast. You muthafuckas are uncouth."

67

"What the fuck's uncouth?" Rocco asks, turning his head to César. Gordo comes back into the room. "He sayin' we're rude and showin' disrespect," Gordo says, checking the curtain and looking outside. César and Rocco exchange a look and laugh.

"At least the fat muthafucka ain't retarted," Beaman spits.

"You've got to be out in ten days," César says, sopping up yolk with the heel of the bread. He stands and pulls a five-dollar bill from his wad.

"The eggs were a bit runny for me but this ought to cover it," he says, tossing the bill on the plate. He walks to the tenant and kicks him hard in the ribs. Beaman coughs.

"Ten days or I come back and snap your spine. Comprendez?"

The trio head for the door.

"I'd like to see you pussies try," Beaman snarls as they leave his apartment.

❖ ❖ ❖

Hell of a story Alexandra laid on me. Now I know what's really up with César and Gan. I need something stronger than beer after that. I go to the kitchen and pull two rock glasses and a bottle of *Booker's Bourbon*. Hand one to Alexandra. We sit side by side on the couch with legs and shoulders touching. We sit in silence. I should push more questions but I need a reprieve. *We* need a reprieve.

This feels like the first moment of quiet since this whole thing began. I like it, especially sitting in my home with a beautiful woman I want to help. I don't want to think about the mess right now or what César and Gan are doing to people who deserve better. Or anything else for that matter.

I grab the remote and play Nat King Cole's *Smile* through the sound system. It may be a corny choice but I don't care. Nat's silky smooth voice goes great with the Booker's flowing through me. I close my eyes. At some point they open and I see Alexandra's hand on my thigh. I hadn't felt her put it there. I wrap my big hand around it. It's small, warm and smooth. I close my eyes again and enjoy the calm before the storm that I will soon inflict on Gan and César.

She pulls her hand from mine. I feel movement beside me and open my eyes. Alexandra eases her leg across my thighs and straddles me. Her long hair flows down and covers one eye. With the other she stares at me. Her intent is obvious. She slowly lowers down and kisses me softly on the lips. I kiss back. We pull apart for a brief moment then her next kiss is not so gentle, neither is mine. Her tongue is warm and tastes of bourbon. I rise. Her legs wrap around me as I slide a hand under her shapely butt. We kiss all the way to the bedroom.

She moans slightly as I lay her on the bed. We work fast at losing our clothes. I lower myself onto her. She winces.

"Sorry, too heavy?"

"No, it's my leg," she says referring to her bullet wound... and dog bite. I'd totally forgotten. I gently roll off and ease her on top. She adjusts her hips and with her hand guides me inside her. She lowers down slowly, pauses with a moan, then lowers the remaining distance.

"Oh my god," she whispers, sucking air in.

I hold her ass at the hips and roll with her easy motion. Her eyes are closed. I watch her, can't take my eyes off her. Slowly her lids lift. She smiles, then comes down and kisses me deeply. She rocks back up and picks up the pace. I caress her firm breasts.

"Yes," she whispers.

We go at it like this, hard and fast. She leans forward and digs her nails into my chest. She rocks faster.

"Ouch, ow," she says.

"Shit, sorry," I say, realizing I grabbed her upper arm at another dog-bite wound.

"It's okay, don't stop, don't… shit, I won't… aah… I won't break."

My hands go back to her butt and I thrust with all I've got. I can't get far enough into this beautiful woman. A high-pitch sound escapes her mouth. She digs her nails in again, deeper this time and stops moving. Her entire body quakes. She's at that point. I move to pull out, knowing I'm about to hit the lotto, but she says no.

"I'm on the pill," she breathes. "Come inside me."

She doesn't have to ask me twice.

❖ ❖ ❖

It wasn't the longest round on record, but we lie still, breathing heavy, with bodies covered in sweat. Neither of us speak. I roll over and kiss her gently.

"That was nice," she says.

"Water?" I ask, getting up. She nods.

When I come back we drink heavily and put the glasses on the bedside tables. She nestles into me as I lie on my back.

"Nice is such a lame word," she says. "I meant to say that was amazing."

"I ain't gonna argue that."

"It's not going to get weird now, is it?"

"Nothin' weird about two consenting adults," I say.

She props her body up on her elbows and smiles at me. "Good, because I hope we can do it again."

"You bet yo' ass we'll—"

"And not just tonight, I mean," she says coyly. I haul her on top of me.

"Not just tonight," I say. The next round we add in the foreplay we'd left out in round one and go at the whole thing more slowly.

I go for more water when we we're done.

"You know, Moose, I realize Jackie and I can be pains in the ass, and I'm sorry for that. We've been through a lot. Like everybody, we have a past. Gan and César aren't the only assholes we've come up against."

"The monsters you mentioned earlier. Expand on that."

"I will, but not now. I need to sleep, you're almost too much for me."

"Too much, huh?"

"I said almost."

"I have to shower and get to the club. I promised Grimes I'd swing by and help them close. We gotta private party—first time clients. Somethin' 'bout 'em's got Grimes nervous—says they kinda shady."

"Let me use the bathroom first." She hops naked out of the bed.

I hear her phone buzz. I glance at the screen and read, "Mom." I'm about to take the phone to her but the call ends. Her mother must have hung up. The phone is unlocked. I go to her contacts and scroll down to "Mom."

The number has the 626 area code, which is not Mexico, it's primarily the San Gabriel Valley. Back in the day, it was all 818 but then split off in 1997, due to growth. I feel like I'm being played again. As water flushes in the bathroom, I check the full contact info and get an address in West Covina, California. I hear the tap running. I've got maybe ten seconds before she comes out. I share the contact info to my phone, then put hers back down.

She walks out and my anger subsides about the possibility of being lied to, again. From head to toe she's a vision. She walks over with a flirtatious smile, stands on her tiptoes and kisses me. I put my hand to the small of her back, haul her in and lengthen the kiss.

"Your turn," she says, and does a little hop to her clothes. She grins at me as she slowly shimmies into her panties. I kiss her again then hit the shower.

❖ ❖ ❖

Next morning, I'm up and out the door. Traffic is too heavy for my liking. It ain't quite what we Angelenos call a parking lot but it isn't far off. Dragging thirty miles an hour on the freeway means it's going to be twice as slow on the surface streets.

I practically need a translator to filter through the stories the sisters keep feeding me, which is why I want to see for myself if their mother is already in L.A. or in Mexico. I don't believe the girls' lies come from malice, which is why I still deal with them. I feel they fabricate out of fear, or survival, and I'll bet the deed to the home grandma left me that their habitual lying goes way back.

Peeling back the layers to their lying past is not the mystery I want to solve, or even have time to solve, but if I can get something from their mother, then maybe I could read the girls a little better. Knowing them better might give me an advantage over Gan because I need every edge I can get.

I frequently check my mirror for a tail—all clear. Occasionally I peep the rides around me. It's an old football habit. You always have a head on a swivel otherwise ya get blindsided. An Asian woman in a green Jetta fixes her eyeliner. Two Latino gardeners in a small Japanese pickup laugh at something the driver is explaining into his hand-held cell phone. Hands flailing, an unnatural blond driving a black Tesla shouts at her partner—trouble in paradise. A massive guy in a town car, wearing a chauffeur's hat two sizes too small stares straight ahead. He's the only one focused on the driving task at hand.

I crawl along for another hour, and by now, I've run three different strategies for dispatching Gan and his heavies. As my exit looms, I slide three lanes to my right. The town car from earlier is two car lengths ahead and apparently taking the same exit. After making the off-ramp I'm at the alleged Lopez momma's home. There's no car in front and no signs of life in the small, single-family house. It's possible someone's inside or in the backyard, but it doesn't feel that way. Sometimes it's as though an empty house talks to you, let's you know nobody's home.

I wait, with no particular time limit as to how long. Up and down the block neighbors come and go. Many holler from cars to porches and back. So far, the big brother sitting in the pickup truck hasn't drawn any suspicion, which is good. Twenty minutes ease by before a four-year old Japanese compact pulls up. Hazard lights flash. A Latina woman in her late fifties, early sixties, gets out of the passenger side. She opens the back and hauls two grocery bags out. After thanking the woman driver around the same age, she heads for the house—but not before showing me a full shot of her face.

It's Alexandra and Jackie's mother, undeniably. Her hair is shorter, and she's a little shorter and rounder, but it's her. She could even pass as the eldest sister. The moment she gets her front door open, I get out, enter the tiny yard through the low wooden gate and mount the steps. I knock immediately, hoping she'll assume I'm her friend who just dropped her off, and open the door up without thinking. That way, there'll be no peeking through peep holes or calling out, 'Who is it?'

"Hola, oh—I thought you were—"

"Mrs. Lopez?"

"Si."

"My name's Doug McCrae. I'm friends with your daughters Alexandra and Jackie. We're actually workin' on something. Mind if I come in for a quick chat?"

"Oh, I don't know," she says, moving a hand to her neck as if clutching the lapels of a bathrobe together.

"If you want, you can call them. I don't mind waiting. I'd like to talk to you."

Her eyes narrow to slits as she studies me.

"No, it's okay. Your *ojos* they are kind. Please come in."

"Thank you," I say, stepping into her spit-shine clean home. "I saw you come in with the bags. Can I help you carry anything?"

"Not necessary, but please, come this way."

We leave her small living room and walk down a tight hallway. On my left is a tiny powder room. The wall on the right has family pictures. I spot the girls at various stages in time, but don't linger too long. We enter a small kitchen. She has me sit at her little kitchen table. I offer to help a second time but she denies me and puts her articles away.

Once finished, she extends her hand, "I am Rosarita, *mucho gusto*, Doug." I shake and insist she call me Moose. She opens a fridge that looks to be twenty years old and pulls out two small bowls covered in plastic wrap.

"Moose, could you reach up in that cupboard above the stove and grab the tortilla chips, please?"

"Of course," I say, hearing my stomach get excited.

"Gracias, that way I don't have to get my little stool out. Put them on the kitchen table."

We sit and have small talk over bowls of salsa and guacamole.

"This guac' must be homemade. Best I ever had," I say.

She offers me a beer, which is my favorite accompaniment with chips and guac but tell her I need to drive back to L.A. and settle on water.

"So, this is nice but…" Her look turns serious. "What exactly are you working on with my girls?"

"I'm helping Alexandra. Job related."

"Ah, Mr. Gan, big man of the campus," she sneers, in a voice rich with disdain.

"Not a fan?"

"*No me gusta*. But my daughter has a job, paying her bills, so I am happy."

The words sound like a mantra she uses to put herself at ease. Her face suddenly changes.

"Is she okay? Has Gan done something?"

"Oh no, she's fine," I say, not answering her second question. I dip another chip in the guac.

"How long have you lived in West Covina?"

"Thirty years or so, why?" she asks, with a hint of suspicion.

"The girls are pooling their resources."

"Oh?"

"Yes, they gonna to pay a coyote to bring someone across the border at Texas."

Rosarita sits back and slaps the table with a laugh. "Nonsense, who are they bringing over the border?"

"Their mother. At least that's what they told me."

Rosarita shakes her head back and forth.

"Could they be talkin' 'bout a step mother?" I ask, knowing the answer.

She stands up, spins the chair around to face the opposite direction, then sits facing me with her elbows on the chair back.

With a heavy sigh she says, "My girls are very close, very, very close. Sometimes they cook up stories."

"I've noticed. Why?"

"It was not easy for the girls when they were growing up. A mother does what she can. She does her best, but she's young." Her eyes grow distant. We sit quietly. All that can be heard is the neighbor's lawn mower.

Finally... "Do you have kids, Moose?"

"No."

"Well, if that day comes, make sure that whatever demons you have are destroyed before you brings *ninos* into this world."

"I hear that," I say. "Rosarita, my main job is nightclub bouncer. Most people think we're big, dumb, slow-moving objects. But we become great observers. Great listeners too."

"Si, okay."

"On top of that, my grandmother, *mi abulela,* always told me to listen and learn." Rosarita nods in agreement.

"You say a mother does her best for her children. Then you say we should slay our demons before having children."

Rosarita stares down into her hands. We both know what is coming.

"Who's the demon that hurt yo' kids Rosarita? Who couldn't you protect them from?"

Tears slowly roll down both cheeks. She still works at her hands.

"I'm gonna take a shot and guess it was their father. He abused them, didn't he?"

She barely nods. Tears come harder and her body shakes. She seems to shrink in size before me. I get up and put a hand on her shoulder. She squeezes my hand with hers.

"You were probably barely twenty years old when you had Jackie right? You were young and probably had no idea what—"

"A mother is supposed to protect the ninas," she shouts. "By the time I found out it was too—"

"You are not to blame. He's the demon, not you. Your daughters are strong and doing fine in this world and that's because of you, their mother."

She lets go of my hand and buries her face in both hands. I sit back down and give her a moment. I like Rosarita. I feel for her. Now I want to protect the entire Lopez family. The sobbing subsides. She wipes at her tears and asks if I really like her homemade guacamole.

"Like I said before, the best I've ever had."

She forces a smile. "Gracias, Moose." She pushes the bowl towards me. I appreciate the gesture. We sit and chat like old friends. She runs down the girls' childhoods through teenage years, including the three tragic years her former husband sexually abused her daughters. As she covers this ground, my water glass breaks in my hand.

"I am so sorry, Ms. Lopez," I say, picking up shards of glass from the table and tile floor.

"*Ay dios mio*, are you okay, Mr. Moose?"

"Yes, sorry about the glass."

She checks my hand and to our surprise there are no cuts.

"Your ex—the monster, is he still alive?" I ask with phony casualness.

The shrewdness in her eye reads me like a book.

"He is dead, so you can relax, you don't need to—"

"Glad to hear it." Her knowing look reads that I'd have hunted him down if he were still alive. She grabs the empty guacamole bowl and asks if I'd like more.

"Thank you but I've got to get back on that damn freeway."

She walks me to the door and unlocks the deadbolt.

"Handle this the way you like but please don't tell the girls I speak to you about their father—unless you absolutely must."

"Certainly. Thanks for the food and conversation, Ms. Lopez."

"Rosarita," she says, and pulls me into a tight hug. "Come visit me again, anytime. And please, protect my girls."

❖ ❖ ❖

I work my way back to the freeway, then join the rest of the slow-moving freeway cattle. It takes three minutes to cross all lanes to the fast lane. A new burning question has just been added to the pile of unknowns: what do the girls really need the thirty large for? As I play out the upcoming dialogue, something bumps my train of thought. A black town car is two car-lengths up ahead and one lane over. I always listen to my triggers. I try and move up. The license plate doesn't help since I didn't commit it to memory earlier. However, the driver's head is large, and the chauffeur's hat is *still* too small. One thing I learned long ago, a good tail can happen in front of your vehicle as well as from the rear. The front tail is more difficult and runs a higher risk of the tail being spotted, but most people don't expect a tail up-front. It's counterintuitive.

This phony car-service driver tailed me to Rosarita's, sat on me and is following me now, up ahead. There's a familiarity to the driver, even though I haven't clearly seen his face. It bugs me. I rack my brain, inching closer. I move to his right—one lane separates us. I stay back on his hip. He'll have to crane his neck to see me. The recognition hits me like an illegal block in the back by a three hundred pound lineman from the blindside—I don't need to see his face. It's the size of his head and neck that jog my memory. It's the Samoan, Fetu—Gan's oversized gatekeeper.

There's no play here on the freeway, I'll just head toward home then tail him until he scrams. If he doesn't blow and pulls over, then him and me will settle our thing in the street. I dig out my phone and dial Alexandra.

"Hey Moose, any news?"

"Yo' gonna be pissed but try and hold it. Things are movin' Mach 10. Gan's big Samoan dude, Fetu, tailed me out to your mother's. I'm coming back from there now."

"What? My mother's—"

"In West Covina. I'm coming back now." Alexandra starts to talk but I cut her off.

"Listen, either she needs to stay somewhere other than her house, or someone who knows how to handle theyself needs to stay with her for at least seventy-two hours. Cool?"

"Oh my god. How did you find my mother?"

"Doesn't matter. Her safety does. You need to handle this for her."

" I know someone who can stay with her. But we need to talk."

"We talkin' now. D' ya know when the next dog fight pops off?"

"Tomorrow."

"Good, now listen carefully. We're going to that fight. You, me, and your sister."

"Huh?"

"We're gonna to end this thing, get you yo' money and take care of two assholes."

"Moose, you're going too fast. Aren't you going to ask me about the thirty thousand?"

"Yeah, so prepare yo' answer for later. Ya got a motel or somewhere y'all can crash other than home?"

❖ ❖ ❖

The Samoan maintains his distance. I hold my speed, then move to the slow lane four miles before my intended exit. I give him a clear signal. He bites and hits the exit a car length ahead of me. He slows at the bottom of the ramp. He could make the light but lightens up, waiting on my turn signal. The car immediately behind him lays on the horn and flips him the bird. My signal is easy to see, being that it's on my big side-mirror as well as on the bumper.

The light turns green. Fetu makes the right and moves into the far right lane. He passes one side street. I take the next without signaling and make a hard right. He's got two choices, either drop the tail or go up a block, make the next right, then another, and look for me. I drive barely five miles an hour down the side street. Cars are parked on the left side of me. A midsize sedan pulls up behind and gives me a toot. I wave her past. She gives me another toot of disapproval. I'm two-thirds down the block when the town car rounds the corner. We're grill to grill with twelve feet of space between us. He stops. He looks surprised. I roll forward until our expressions are clearly readable. My eyes are as dead as his.

The horn of a vehicle blasts me from behind. I'm straddling the road so he can't pass. I roll forward another foot. The Samoan holds his ride in place. His face remains as empty as mine. I continue to move forward. My truck is practically on top of him now. With a foot to go, I punch it and ram his grill. A crumbling of metal—there's a high-pitch ping sound as a piece of his bumper hits the pavement. The car behind me honks continuously. I'll have to move soon, before they call the cops.

The Samoan is unfazed by our fender bender. Nothing moves on his large face as he slowly eases his transmission into reverse. He backs up to the end of the block without so much as a glance into his rearview or side-mirror. I keep pace with him until he cranks his wheel at the intersection and backs into the street. A Porsche Panamera is forced to lock its brakes up. Fetu doesn't flinch. He comes to a stop.

I pull straight into the intersection and stare at him out the driver's window. We hold our spots a moment longer before I see his hand move to the gearshift. He punches it, attempting to T-bone me. I'm way ahead of him. My tires scream but catch asphalt immediately. I catapult through the intersection. His twisted grill misses my back end by inches. He speeds through the intersection. I check my mirror but know full well he's gone. Today's playoff game is done, but we'll meet in the final.

❖ ❖ ❖

"Alexandra, is Jackie with you?"

"Yup, you're on speaker."

"Good, here's how it's gon' go."

"How about you tell us why you went to visit our mother?" Jackie demands. "You ever hear of boundaries?"

"Take it easy, Jackie," Alexandra says.

"When the people I work with go blurrin' the lines then *I* set the boundaries. I knew that Mexico-coyote story was bullshit before you finished tellin' it, but I needed to verify. Now tell me what the money is for."

"Familia, as in it's none of your—"

"We need the money for meds!" Alexandra shouts, over her sister.

"What the fuck, Alexandra?" Jackie loud-whispers.

"There, now you know. A family member has a blood disease. It's rare. The medication used to be doable, but the pharmaceutical company was sold to another company. And guess what they did?"

"No doubt jacked the price of the drug."

Jackie jumps in "Jacked? No my friend, a four hundred and fifty percent increase is not jacked, it's extortion. Believe me, I've been in jail with hard bitches who wouldn't even do something like this if they were in charge. The meds now come out at nearly sixty grand a year—a year, Moose!"

She lets out a long litany of Spanish curse words after the mention of my name. Alexandra tries to calm her sister, and for half a minute the two of them argue back and forth in a mixture of English and Spanish. I have to shut it down.

"Enough. I get it, you're pissed, and rightfully so. I'm in the deep water on this thing and I have a plan. When the dust settles y'all should have enough money to put with yo' original thirty to cover a year, maybe six months more on top But it only works if you stop bullshitting and follow my lead. *Entiendas,* dammit?"

The girls quietly thank me and say they understand.

"Why did y'all feed me the fake mother over-the-border story?"

"Health issues are very personal, Moose. It is the business of the familia, *comprendez*?"

❖ ❖ ❖

That night at the club, I interrupt Grimes in his office. I 'shh' him as he's watching a segment on the local news that piques my interest. Gan has officially announced his run for mayor. There's a montage of Gan looking over various building projects, sometimes in a hard hat, other times looking over blueprints. Soon, they'll have footage of him ducking into the back of a cop car with news of his dogfighting. My phone vibrates with a text. It's Alexandra.

Will you be home soon?

You bet.

Home alone?

One of those rare times, yeah.

Want some company?

❖ ❖ ❖

We lay back, both staring at my ceiling. The clock reads two-thirty a.m. Alexandra lies naked beside me.

Out of the blue, I decide to chance it. "So... who's the family member needs the meds?"

She doesn't move. "Me," she says simply.

"You don't look sick."

"That's why they call it medication. It's medicates the illness."

Words fail me. It's the truth, I can hear it.

"They're working on a cure," she says. "I'm young, I can beat this."

I roll over and hug her close.

"Why are you hanging in bars doing the bouncing thing?" Now she's the one with the question.

"It's the kinda gig you get offered when you're this size. But I don't just bounce, I do executive protection every now and then, as well. That's where the real dough lives."

"Why not do that full-time?"

I lock up briefly, then decide to hell with it.

"I hurt someone real bad, nearly killed him. I was protecting an ex-NFL player. He has a girl in a hotel room. I hear screams, fight through the other security detail, and snatch the girl out of there. Naturally, I got fired but it left a foul taste in my mouth."

"So, was the NFL guy the one you hurt?"

"Wasn't planning on it but later I found out the girl was underage. So I looked a little deeper at it and find out her family was paid off to keep quiet. Family was poor and took the fifteen K and walked."

"What? Fifteen K, that's it?"

"Which is why I waited two months, tracked him down. I broke his leg and a couple o' ribs. I was going to leave it at that when he asked why was I doing it to him. When I mentioned the girl, he said things about her, things I won't repeat. So," I sigh, "I cracked a couple vertebrae in his neck. He lived, but it was further than I wanted to take it. I just lost it."

"Did you get an assault charge?" she asks quietly.

"Nobody came for me. He never talked."

"Wow, why wouldn't he talk?"

"I asked him not to."

"Oh," she says, getting the picture.

I put a finger under her chin and tilt her face up.

"Now I bounce and only take exec gigs, freelance. I'm choosy. I also do the occasional freebie, as you know," I say, and kiss her. "But I'm putting some money together for a little project."

"Ooh, what is it?"

"You and Jackie aren't the only ones with secrets, babe," I say, kissing her, again.

❖ ❖ ❖

The next morning, I make bacon, eggs and coffee for us. Alexandra is shocked that I eat five eggs.

"Today's a big day, need my strength," I say. "Make sure your phone is with you and fully charged. Tonight, I need you and Jackie to dress in black—all black. But make sure you both wear white long-sleeve tops over the black. No loose clothing, nothing that can get caught up on anything." She nods.

"And footwear is key— think something you can move fast in, I'm talking a flat-out sprint. A cross-trainer would be good, especially for Jackie. She'll be navigating trails."

Alexandra nods again, knowing not to interrupt with questions at this point.

"Also, how about carrying a gun?"

She shakes her head back and forth, "Absolutely not. No."

"I thought so."

I walk to the cabinet my violin lives in, and pull the top drawer open. I hold both sides of the drawer evenly because sometimes it pops off the track. I pull a slim wooden case from the drawer, open it, and let Alexandra have a look.

"Chopsticks?"

"Mm hmm."

"They're beautiful," she says, gently removing them from the case. "What do the characters mean?"

"Tranquility."

She tests the heft. "These look like wood but they're not—so light."

"Aluminum," I tell her.

She runs a slender hand down the stick, feeling the embossed characters.

"Careful of the point," I tell her, as her hand nears the end. She gently tests the point with her pinky finger and lets out a quiet whistle.

"My grandma's. She had varying tastes for things all over this world."

"Beautiful," she says a second time, putting the chopsticks back in the case.

"Can you work these into your hair and make it look like an up-do?"

"I could, why?"

"You ain't carrying a gun, so you'll carry these. If this goes south, these will be your weapons. I know yo' sister will carry, so don't try and talk her out of it."

Her face flushes with concern. "Oh my god," she says plopping on a counter stool. I put a hand to her shoulder.

"You scared. That's aight. Harness it and you'll come out on top."

With a determined look she straightens her back, pulls the chopsticks, and works her hair up three different ways. Satisfied, I take the next five minutes to show her vital target points on the head and body, if an opponent pushes her into a corner.

"Okay," she says with a sigh. "Gimme the rest of the plan."

"In time."

Her brow furrows, "Are you always this controlling?"

"*In* control, not controlling. There's a difference."

I move to the fridge and pour two glasses of ice tea. She takes one, as if on autopilot.

"Look, since our lives have been thrown together we been movin' closer to the end zone, yard by yard. Yo' first angle was a blackmail play, which we know wouldn't have worked. Here's the plan: After we rob Gan, we send that letter wide, and hip the cops to the fights. His run for mayor is over. Best case he does time for the dogs. But if he only gets fines and community, he'll be on the law's radar. He'd be a fool to take a run at you."

Alexandra sits quietly and takes it all in. I give her a moment before adding, "And you and your sister go free with money in your pockets."

She eases off the stool, stands on her tiptoes and kisses me gently on the lips.

❖ ❖ ❖

"Welcome to Uncle Sam's Copies, how can I help you?"

"Hi Sheila," I say, clocking her name tag. "I need to replicate what's in this picture, then I need to laminate it."

She takes the phone from me and looks at the photo.

"No problem, we can do those colors and, oh, what are the dimensions?"

"Length is five and a half inches, width is four."

"Great. Are you going with the lanyard?"

"Most def. I will need the holes in the plastic where the clips attach. Is that doable? If not, I'll need you to leave the plastic a little long and I'll cut the holes myself."

"We can do that, easy. How many do you want done?"

"Three sets oughtta do it."

The sitting area reminds me of a muffler-shop waiting area. They even have the cheap coffee, tasting like it was brewed last week, on a hot plate. I sit down and call Jackie to confirm all my instructions.

"White with black underneath, shoes I can haul ass in, and my piece."

"Cool, pick you up at ten-fifteen."

Sheila waves me over ten minutes later to look at the product before she seals it in plastic. I dump my muddy coffee, join her at the desk, and pull up my picture of the lanyard to compare it to her replica. It looks good at first eyeball, but then I look longer, the way security might.

"I think we good," Sheila.

❖ ❖ ❖

I fire up my truck and point it toward the Home Depot where they sell six-foot wooden dowels, three quarters of an inch in diameter. I take my dowel to the cutting bench and cut two feet off with the small-tooth handsaw they make available to customers. I test-wield the four-foot section and the weight feels good. Leaving the lumber department, I move to the hooks-and-fasteners aisle, grabbing an inch and a half metal hook with a screw at the back end. Before reaching home, I pit-stop at Silverlake Toy and Costume. I'm home twenty minutes later.

❖ ❖ ❖

Alexandra and Jackie are flopping at the Lido Motel; no pool, no pets, no loitering. I text them when I'm out front at the curb. They come out dressed the way I asked. They climb in. I approve of Alexandra's look, then crane around and check Jackie out.

"Say hello to my little friend," she says, lifting her top to reveal a Smith and Wesson nine-milli in her waistband. I give her a short nod.

"So?" Jackie asks, with expectant eyes. "What's the plan?

"Gan has decided to eat the thirty K he loaned Alexandra."

"Whaa—?"

"Generous guy, huh?"

"No, that doesn't sound like—"

"He plans Alexandra not being around very long. That means we have to take him out. Now."

"Take him out?" Jackie quavers. "You mean kill him?"

"Nah, not that way. I've met the dude, he's a narcissistic psychopath. When Alexandra copied his email, it put him over the edge. Your co-worker, Jerry, confirmed that in his voicemail. Gan sent César after you but failed. That stunt will ruin his reputation if we play this right. Might even arrange a little jail time for him.

The women look at each other. I continue.

"When I went out to the fights the other night, I noticed that some of the guards take bets, have 'em counted, and then drop off the cash at Gan's limo. Tonight, we hit that car."

"How are we supposed to pull that off?"

I pull out the lanyards and hand them over. "We cause a little pandemonium, first. And Jackie, we're going with a disguise for you." I hand over a close-cropped wig and thick glasses."

"Why the disguise? They don't know me," she says, taking the items.

"Because you look too much like your sister. We don't want them grabbing you, thinking you're Alexandra."

She purses her lips, considering.

"What about me?" Alexandra says.

"You be squeezing into my lockbox, y'all are tiny enough."

"Are you serious? What if they open the box?"

"They won't, but if they push it, I'll tell 'em I don't have that key with me. Which I won't, cause Jackie will have it."

She makes a face but doesn't fuss as I give her sister the key.

"Gan's men will be stationed at a gate that leads to the parking lot. These laminates and lanyards will get us inside."

❖ ❖ ❖

Headin' into the fourth quarter. On the freeway, the lights of Los Angeles wink around us. Once there, we pull within twenty yards of the rear car in the lineup. Jackie makes a final adjustment to the wig I've given her. Hard men at the gate with automatic weapons interview guests through vehicle windows. One asks questions and checks the laminates while the other does a full lap around the vehicle, shining his flashlight into windows and under chassis. He's looking for stowaways and any artillery heavier than a handgun.

Far beyond is an area with extra guards where trucks are parked with steel cages bolted to their beds. Inside the cages are fighting dogs. Anger wells up as I see the brutality used in unloading the dogs by the owners. On short, heavy chains, some dogs are whipped with thick leather straps, some kicked, the kind of abuse that little men believe is control. Most of it is show for other owners. I feel my jaw clench along with my fists. Part of me wants to change the plan and take out the dog owners instead. I breathe deep and exhale slowly.

An Audi Q7 goes through inspection before it's our turn.

"You good?" I say quietly to Jackie. Eyes forward, she says a quick 'Mm hmm.'

The perimeter guard circles the truck and shines his heavy-duty flashlight in and over my truck. We ignore him and focus on the guard asking to see our laminates. He's satisfied with mine and asks Jackie to pass hers over. He's got a Tec-9 semi-auto slung over his shoulder. He frowns at the laminate, then shoots Jackie a hard look. I ready myself for this to go south. I have my hand on the door handle. I'll open the door into his body, disarm him, and hope like hell I can use his gun to make the other guard give up his weapon. Mission unaccomplished…but at least we'll get away with our asses in one piece.

"What's the fucking problem?" Jackie asks, glaring through the thick glasses.

I grip the door handle. He flips the laminate over. My heart ticks up a notch—I can't remember if there was any text or logos on the back. Did Sheila check this? Wound up tight, I'm ready to spring. He tosses the laminate across me to Jackie.

"No problem, move ahead," he says. "And watch your fucking mouth, four-eyes."

Jackie flinches. I put a hand on her lap and steady her.

We pull to the far end of the lot, but not too close to the heavily guarded dog-owner area. I lower the tailgate. Jackie reaches over the lip of the truck from the passenger side and sticks the key in the lockbox. Alexandra is out in seconds and on the gravel beside us. She gives no complaint. I respect that.

We join the other guests. These are the kind of guys I'd bar entry from my club just by eyeballing them—tatted up, greasy haired assholes and skinheads, over-built dudes on their third steroid cycles. Shirts, sweaters and waistbands bulge everywhere. Everyone is armed. It would probably be more trouble than it's worth for the guards to confiscate pieces from this crowd, which suits me fine. The coolness of my Glock is at the small of my back. We move like factory workers heading to dead-end jobs. Menacing glances move left and right with veiled threats. Testosterone is on tilt. The Lopez sisters draw glances but nothing lingering. These men know not to trespass.

Gan's limo is to my right near the rear tent. The motorhome is to our left—we veer toward it. The group is uninterested in our detour. Their focus is the upcoming brutality and the prospect of fattening the wallet The three of us gather at the end of the motorhome, furthest from the amphitheater. Crowd volume is up with anticipation.

"Lose the white tops and that disguise," I whisper.

"Glad to, I look like a fucking dyke in this shit," Jackie says, tossing the gear to the dirt.

"Stay back of the amphitheater and head up that hill. Those sugar-bush shrubs will give you cover."

I open my bag and pull out the homemade dowel and hook. "You're gonna find the dog kennel at the top of the hill. Avoid the guard and climb onto the kennel roof. There's a ladder. Lean over the lip and unlatch the cages to let them suckas out. They'll take care of the pandemonium part."

"Let 'em out, my ass, they'll rip me to shit!"

"Nah. You'll be too high for them to jump. Besides, they'll head straight for the fights and the smell of blood."

Once you feel undetected, haul ass like your life depends on it. Your sister n' me can't hide here for long."

Without a word, she gives her sister a firm hug, then takes off.

We watch her clear the amphitheater. No one pays attention because the first fight has begun. With our backs to the wall, I feel Alexandra's body tremble.

"Are you all right?" I move closer to her. She nods with eyes closed. The dogs' growls and crowd noise is too much. In her mind, she's back on the pavement outside my house. Like a fool I hadn't considered this.

"Are you sure, because we could—"

"Yes," she snaps.

I squeeze her hand but she yanks it away. I slide around the corner to peek at the fight. I pull out my phone and quickly fire off a text. Putting it away, I see César is in the middle of the ring with a thickly built pit bull on a short leash. The dog's opponent is the same size but not nearly as muscular. I know some fighting-dog owners feed their dogs steroids. I have no doubt César has juiced his dog.

The dogs engage center ring. César's dog bowls the smaller pit over with its big chest and has its throat torn out in seconds. The crowd goes wild. I'm glad Alexandra can't see it from around the corner.

As I move back to her, there's movement in the motorhome.

"Someone's coming," I say, hustling her to the back of the structure. The door opens. A set of feet clomp down the steps. I signal for Alexandra to shimmy under the big vehicle. She does without a sound. I'll never fit. One of Gan's guards rounds the corner.

"Whoa, what the fuck you doin' back here man?"

I raise my hands revealing a cell phone in one hand. "Calling my boss, gotta place a bet."

"Ya can't be back here, dude. Back to the pit, or I'm tossin' ya."

"You got it, bud," I say. "Just let me make this call or it's my ass."

He points a Browning Hi-Power at my chest. "Final warning, asshole."

He doesn't notice Alexandra slide, without a sound, from under the motorhome.

"You might get a shot off, but you'll bleed out for sure," Alexandra says calmly from behind him, with both chopstick-points at the carotid artery of his neck. The guard lowers his arm and drops the gun on the ground. Alexandra kicks him squarely in the groin from behind. I walk over, raise my leg high, and stomp him unconscious.

Two gunshots ring out from the kennel area.

"Shit," I say. Alexandra looks at me with wide eyes. We scramble to the end of the motorhome. I check the fights. Patrons' heads turn, trying to track the shots. Alexandra's phone and mine buzz simultaneously. Jackie has sent us a text:

Shots mine. Guard injured- running your way. Letting dogs loose, I'm on my way. It's on!

"We move now," I shout. "Gotta get to that limo before we get caught up with—"

A guard limp-runs down the hill—must be the guy Jackie shot. Two dogs are on his heels. He turns and fires, misses. They haul him down. He's done. The patrons at the amphitheater erupt with panic as more dogs trail behind the downed guard. Two dogs in the pit keep fighting.

Alexandra and I sprint across the open field. Fight fans flood out of the amphitheater. Some are forced into the second tent, Gan's tent. They collide with guards pouring out. The loose dogs attack people and other dogs at random. Guards shoot at marauding dogs

95

but the owners defend their animals and fire on the guards. Bullets zip in every direction.

"Keep your head down," I shout to Alexandra, but she's not behind me. She's gone. I come face to face with one of the guards.

"You're that big fucker Gan warned us about." He smiles as he raises his gun at me. A mastiff-pit mix clamps onto his arm and takes him to the ground. His gun goes off, but the dog has the edge. I leap over both of them and keep moving. Where is Alexandra?

In my peripheral, I see César coming in from my nine o'clock for a second attack. I don't let on I've clocked him. I maintain my pace. He's six feet away. I keep my eyes forward. He closes to within three feet of me. Once he's within striking distance, I halt. His overhand swing with a knife sails past my face as I arch backward. His momentum carries him forward. I grab him from behind and manipulate his knife hand. It looks like suicide as I force his arm toward his body. The knife enters his throat. I wrap my hand around his and give it hard twists in both directions.

I don't so much as look at him as he drops to the ground, gurgling. The limo still seems miles away. I scan the area for Alexandra. Nothing. Jackie's voice catches my ear from behind. I see her move through the chaos, same as me. Our eyes lock. I point to the limo. She nods and then communicates something I don't comprehend—but understanding dawns as I feel something like an anaconda snake wrap itself around my throat. At the end of two thick arms is Fetu, Donnie Gan's Samoan gatekeeper. His high-pitch giggle blends with the sound of distant sirens.

My air is limited while my head pulsates with pain. I kick at his knee, but he checks it. *Think, Moose.* I put both hands on one of his wrists—two against one—and corkscrew my hands back and forth. He giggles more, as he thinks I'm not strong enough to escape his grasp. I quickly eye-poke him, then go back to the wrist.

The grip loosens. Air rushes into my lungs. I manipulate the wrist and shove it toward him, hard-breaking it. I'm not done. I step to the side and move his elbow outward at a forty-five degree angle and snap that too. He balls his free hand into a fist, but by now I'm beside him in a sort of country music style dance step. I put all my weight at the elbow and take him to ground. We land hard. With my back to him, I yank on his arm and hear a crisp 'crack' as his shoulder pops out of the socket. The limb is now useless.

His high-pitch laugh is now a high-pitched scream. I roll out and get to my feet. My Glock's instantly in my hand and spits a bullet in his kneecap. Then I'm back to the mission. Clearing cobwebs, I see Alexandra enter the limo's back door. Cops are now infiltrating the scene. Most guards surrender, but many dog owners decide life isn't worth living without their animal, and going to jail isn't in their plans. They exchange gunfire with the cops. I forge ahead, keeping low. Jackie now parallels me. A heavy rottweiler leaps at her. She puts three into the body but the dog's momentum lays her out. I pull the dead animal off her and move to help her up.

"Forget about me damn it. Keep moving, Moose," she says. Alexandra exits the limo with hair down and frazzled. She staggers along the vehicle, using it for support.

Two dogs kill off a guard and head straight for Alexandra. She sees them and freezes. I curse myself again. Is this PTSD from her previous attack? How could I have been so stupid to bring her here? Jackie and I call to her, but we're not heard. I sprint ahead and fire on the run. It takes me four shots to put one of the dogs down. Jackie gets caught up with a guard and shouts for me to keep going. I fire on the second dog, but keep missing.

The limo's back door opens and Donnie Gan staggers out. My grandmother's chopsticks protrude from his neck. He yanks them out, causing blood to spurt. With one hand on the wound and the other on a Beretta he sees Alexandra and fires two times. *Bang, bang!* She goes down.

"No!"

I take aim at Gan, center mass.

"Don't do it, Moose," Office Ortiz says, with the muzzle of his service weapon at my temple.

"Shoot that dog, Ortiz, it's heading for Alexandra!" I shout.

But I'm wrong. The dog leaps on Gan and mauls him. I drop my Glock and sprint to Alexandra. Jackie pulls up beside me, and shrieks at the vision. We kneel beside Alexandra and cradle her. She's bleeding heavily from her chest and rib cage. Her eyes are wide with fear. Jackie and I put hands on her wounds but we can't stem the tide.

"Get, get the mo-money, give to Ja-Jackie."

"We did, we have the money," I lie. "Don't talk, help's comin'."

"Stay with us, Alexandra," Jackie screams. "Fuck, fuck, fuck."

"Moo… Moose," Alexandra slurs.

"Yes, I'm here, babe, I'm here. You gonna be okay. You got this."

"Moose, I, I—"

And then there is nothing behind her eyes and no breath from her lips. It is the second time this beautiful woman lies wounded on my lap, only this time I can't save her. Jackie collapses across her sister's torso and wails. Supporting Alexandra's head, I gently close her eyelids. Alexandra Lopez is dead.

Epilogue

Men's County Jail, Los Angeles

Ms. Charlotte Lancer, public defender, is a stout, no-nonsense black woman with thin lips that she holds in a serious line. She hardly opens her lips to deliver her monotone.

"So, what am I lookin' at?" I ask the serious lawyer.

"LAPD appreciates you working with Officer Ortiz. Your text from the crime scene supports this, but they have trouble believing that you were up there for the simple task of reporting a crime."

"We'all were concerned citizens 'bout a possible future mayor bein' up to something nefarious. It was our duty to report it."

"That's good. Bullshit, but good. Remember it that way because judges appreciate that sort of colloquy, Mr. McCrae."

"What about Jackie?" I ask. "I don't want her to do any time."

"Speaking of," she says, "This is for you."

She passes me a handwritten note. It's from Jackie Lopez.

Moose,

You probably feel like shit for my sister's death and you should. I appreciate that you used your one phone call to call my momma. That was a stand up move. The cherry on this shit cake is that fucker Gan died from those chopsticks Alexandra jammed into his scrawny neck. That's what Dick Weasel gets for fucking with a Lopez. I miss her so much. I know you do, too but you gotta own your part.

Until you get out, don't drop the soap Bud.

Jackie

I rub my eyes, which suddenly feel itchy. When I open them, my court appointed lawyer is staring at me with lips in a line and eyes questioning.

"Gan's got a tag on his toe, huh?"

"Yes, Mr. McCrae."

I fold Jackie's note and slip it into the chest pocket of my county jumpsuit.

"Remember what I said, Jackie Lopez don't do no time. Not one damn second."

"We'll do our best."

"Some good came out of this. Those damn dog fights have been shut down. And we needn't worry about that scumbag becoming mayor."

"Let's hope the judge sees it that way."

"Mm hmm."

The End

ACKNOWLEDGEMENTS

The team involved in getting this book from idea to print has many players. If I took the time to thank all of you by name, this section of the book would have a higher word count than the book itself. On top of that it would hinder me from getting on to my next "Moose" tale. (Oh yeah, he'll be back!) That being said, big thanks to family, friends and readers!

Massive thanks to my loving wife Sonia, for without you I'd never have made it past the first chapter, babydoll! Thanks to my editor Elaine Ash for pushing me into the noir arena and bolting the door behind me. Thanks to Ismael Tavera, the best police consultant and badass neighbor a guy could ever hope for. Many thanks to cover artist Karen Phillips, for turning my cryptic ideas into gold.

Made in the USA
San Bernardino, CA
16 March 2019